NEFARIA

THE CHRONICLES

OF

NEFARIA

WILLIAM A. COOK

EXPATHOS
Groningen, 9724CP
Netherlands

Original Copyright Registration

259658980

Registered with IP Rights office

Under title: *Buried Alive: a Morality Tale*

Copyright Registration Service

Created Sun., Aug.05, 2007: 20:38

Ref. # 204685934

Copyright as *The Chronicles of Nefaria*

10/01/2007

ISBN 978-90-79778-01-0

Author Portrait: Leah Noelle

Cover Photos: William A. Cook

Cover Designs: Leah Noelle Enterprises

NEFARIA

A

Morality Tale

ACKNOWLEDGEMENTS

I owe a debt of gratitude to my department Chair, Professor David Werner, for his copyediting of the manuscript. His astute concern for detail coupled with his narrative insight made more of this book than my limited vision. But, in addition, I must convey my thanks for comments offered when I spent two days listening to constructive criticism as I carved a Janus pumpkin with my grand daughter in southern Vermont listening as well to the geese heading south. I also sought and was granted an opportunity to have Chris Cook, Editor of Pacific Free Press in British Columbia, review the final manuscript. He did so with care and concern. For that I am most grateful. Finally, respectful thanks to my wife whose instinctive understanding of what gives life to all things in their season gave life to this story.

DEDICATION

To all who have suffered and to all who suffer at the hands of

the deceitful, the ruthless and the deranged.

CONTENTS

INTRODUCTION

Chris Cook

A bitter winter welcomes the annual Sacred Season of Forgiveness and Retribution in William A. Cook's fictional Nefaria. Fading in and out of lucidity, suspended between life and oblivion, the once all-powerful leader lay in a coma, his bodily functions aided by the latest medical machinery. Too sick to rise, and too mean to die, the figure under the thin cerecloth reminds of Greene's Harry Lime, the character whose final interment was resisted, "as if nature were doing its best to reject him." In this case, the frozen leader's condition denies him life, while his odious nature and the sheer weight of his crimes seem too great a burden for even Hell's consideration. He is alone now, none knowing of his moments of motionless awareness, or caring about his fate. Ignored by former colleagues and written off as a lost cause by his celebrity doctors, only his nurse, a lowly member of the despised underclass, remains to minister to the Father of the Nation.

Cook's narrative takes place within a disturbingly familiar world of injustice, brutality, and unbearable human misery. As in the 'real" world, most of the suffering is borne by a population living under the heel of a military occupation that dominates their daily lives. Similar too to our world, the dividing line between occupier and the occupied is determined by race and religion and reinforced by guns, concrete and razor wire. The colonialists of fictional Nefaria have created for the displaced indigenous people a walled ghetto, where every aspect of existence depends on the goodwill of their often capricious jailers. A fragmented remnant of what was once their home, the landscape serves as metaphor for the unnatural existence of the inhabitants on both sides of the ubiquitous barriers that dissect the territory.

Nefaria is also a tale of parallel personal worlds: The stricken leader, doomed to lay comatose and forgotten in a hospital wrestling his demons, and the attendant "angel," whose service to the man singly most responsible for the disaster that has befallen her people is her way of fighting to maintain her humanity. Trapped, the man who engineered and administered the slow erasure of a population has only his life and its litany of transgressions against life to occupy his mind between the sweet ministrations of a nurse who refuses to surrender to hate.

Fact and fiction flicker in this account of the miserable conditions created by a settler society that both demonizes and depends upon the natives it trammels under foot and crushes beneath the iron tread of tanks and bulldozers. We need only to tune in to the nightly news to witness the sorry reality Cook's fiction relates: War, rumours of war, and worst of all, the soul deadening daily cruelty a grinding occupation with no end in sight demands.

Nefaria is an accounting as apt for the bitter betrayal of the planet's promise in our young century, a promise disappointed by war and the occupations, as it is for those trapped in the afflicted non-fictional territories where the worst of human nature routinely plays out. He details the relentless humiliation suffered under a generational occupation that daily murders individuals with impunity while collectively punishing the population, and notes the pursuit of an inexorable push toward the final extermination of an entire people. The victims of the intended genocide also fight; they resist with guns and bombs and rockets and stones, but the real battle is within each individual to preserve the "angels of our better nature." Refusing to descend to the unreasoned hatred that drives the endless cycle of hate, oppression and destruction, the young nurse's devotion to her higher angels is the only roadmap out of the morass; she is exemplar and her resistance is the only hope for our and Nefaria's future.

As the winter of George W. Bush's disastrous tenure approaches, new wars and killings vie for headline space with the older horrors we've become mainly inured to. Those "regular" daily outrages against humanity allowed to continue year after year, son after father after son cannot be forgotten, but neither can they be reduced to the simplicity of diametrical opposed positions.

This is not a Shakespeare tragedy, with actors familiarly enstaged: Villain and victim locked in a passion play that mutually defines and destroys them both. What William A. Cook has created is a reflection of a reality too searing for the trivial attentions of politicians and network newsreaders. It is more than merely another cri de coeur for the downtrodden of Iraq and Afghanistan and Palestine, and the too many elsewheres people are systematically brutalized. It is an urgent appeal in defense of how we define humanity, and a prayer that, like the better angel embodied by the caring nurse, it is not too late to salvage our collective soul and move finally towards the long-elusive fulfillment of the human promise.

And as for the dictators and their enablers, Cook suggests we: "Let their respective shadows fall over the wastelands they have created in their arrogance that we may learn and dream once again."

[Chris Cook is a contributing editor to the news web site, Pacific Free Press. He's also a ten year broadcast veteran whose program, Gorilla Radio, is broad/webcast from the University of Victoria in British Columbia, and still clings to the notion human beings are inherently good.]

THE CHRONICLES OF NEFARIA

A MORALITY TALE

Prelude

No one forecast the severe cold as the country entered the sacred season of forgiveness and retribution at year's end. It came suddenly. Even now a light snow falls in swirls from the black sky casting a silent shroud about the hospital. Inside, the Patient lies immobile on the hospital bed, his face pale as marble, the stretched folds of sheets carved like a cerecloth, his form so absolutely still it resembles the medieval sarcophagus prepared for Pope Alexander IV in 1261. But this is not the thirteenth century. It is now, though now may mean nothing to him as he lies there in a coma induced by the cancer that had crept through his body over the years, a cancer that finally took root in his brain and closed down his body. Yet, through the silence of the respirator, he breathes still, imperceptibly, for thirteen months now, a veritable corpse laid out in the viewing parlor of a funeral home. Nothing moves. Silence covers the room like a pall. The darkness of the late evening shrouds the barren trees and only the lonely wail of the wind laments the fallen hero who lives on beyond death itself.

The Season of Forgiveness and Retribution recognizes the finality of life as recorded in the *Book of Judgment*, an ancient text of the Nefarian faith, a finality celebrated at the culmination of the lunar year as it calls on the faithful to remember and contemplate the sinful acts they have committed against their neighbors, friends, and kin. The inauguration of the sacred days began with the establishment of the state of Nefaria, though few knew its origins and none asked. Nefaria exists as it has for centuries in the minds of those who wander the wind swept hills and valleys of the middle kingdoms, remembering ancient civilizations that glistened momentarily in the blazing sun, then faded from view as the eternal sands covered them under layers of silt and forgotten memories. Yet from time to time in ages past, the very wind that buried the might and wisdom of one civilization bared its remains buried deep beneath the sand and uncovered in sealed earthen jars the voices of its prophets that predicted its ineluctable end. But prophetic warnings proffer no wisdom, they become rather the germinating seed for yet one more attempt at glory, one more futile effort to establish personal greatness, one more stab at imposing new ideologies on old beliefs before they are, in their turn, buried beneath the windswept hills waiting the birth, once again, of the next pretender to eminence.

****

Preparation for the season begins early in the fall; ministers spread out from the Worship Hall of the Almighty, the central assembly hall of the church in the holy city of Desperia, to all the outlying parishes with newly crafted verses from the *Book of Judgment* for the Pilgrims that become the solemn chants of the season and with the year's themes for each of the seven days that carry the imprimatur of the Perfect that reigns supreme in the church.

This year, in sympathetic recognition of the declining state of the country's esteemed leader, who lies not "in state," but in a coma at the state hospital, the themes focus on his accomplishments over the past 50 years that have led Nefaria to such a renowned position in the world as a result of his character and virtues. He has become the embodiment of Nefarian virtues and values, a veritable icon of its morality.

He, of course, knows nothing of these developments having fallen into the coma months ago, but he has celebrated the season his entire life and knows the duty of every lay person to seriously address the sins one has inflicted on others. Indeed, as he lies in his coma, the irony of his reality is known to no one; he moves in and out of consciousness able to hear, remember, and contemplate all that has happened in his life but able to communicate nothing to any person.

Ah, my angel has arrived. Angel, indeed. Such a job she has, to lift this fat carcass so fresh sheets can be laid. And I can't even feel it, but it must be done; it's hospital routine. God knows I've been around these places long enough. Bathe the patient, change the sheets, check the monitors. It's routine. But I hear her, hear the door open, her steps, the cloth dropped in the water; why can't I feel her, the water, any god damned thing? Nothing moves. I'm buried alive listening to sounds and idiots.

That noise ... someone else is here. Who? What fool comes now? I hear ... they don't know. That ignorance opens their mouths and they pour their stupidity into the air. "We have to cut, the pressures too great, we have no choice. It may help; if it doesn't, nothing's changed." Fools! Idiots! How strange to hear thoughts whispered about me, when someone can carve into my skull without my consent or mock or curse me when I cannot move.

I hear yet I have no life; everything flows around in sound: the silence, the warm air from the vent, the noise of a car on gravel, the boom of a jet engine, wind outside the window, voices, so many voices, booming ones from down the hall, soft ones like Humilia's, harsh ones that demand she do this or that, voices I'd like to stifle. Sound, sound only sound. What reality is that? No response; I can make no response. I'm alone, so alone. Oh, if I could only see! Even move a finger, utter a sound, anything to show I'm here, alive, conscious ... to touch another.

Few spoke unfavorably of the Patient while he survived surgery after surgery in a vain quest to bring him back to consciousness. But while the surgeons were able to cut out the malignant tumors and stem the cancerous spread, the strokes he suffered left him paralyzed and immobile. The nurses, doctors, interns and aides that attended him could not tell if he had any awareness of his condition or even if he could hear the noises that enveloped him. They knew he could not see or touch or smell; no vital signs were manifest, only the constant click of the monitored heart beat. But hearing remained an unknown as did consciousness. This mystery hovered over the bed and the prostrate body of the Patient; it seeped into the consciousness of all who entered the room imposing a shroud of silence lest he wake and rise from his marble burial bed and curse those who dared speak ill of him. All presumed that he had no sense or cognitive recognition, and in time all acted as though that were true when in his presence.

But the Patient's anguished yearnings reach no ears; he is but another object in the room, as lifeless as the bed stand and chair, something to be moved if needed to mop the floor or reset the monitor. The presence the Patient heard was the cleaning girl, a friend of Humilia's from her neighborhood inside the Wall. Carita is a small girl, not more than five feet tall. Her face is haloed by her black hijab that hangs over her shoulders offering muted but stark contrast to her long grey shalwar that gathers about her shoes. As she enters, she nods to Humilia and motions her to the window away from the bed.

"What is it, Carita, what's wrong?" Humilia's tone conveys the visceral reaction a child born under the occupation feels at the slightest hint of trouble, the anticipation of discrimination or worse.

"Nothing's wrong, I just wanted to know if you saw the Pilgrims on Ypocrisis Street going to the worship hall? There were hundreds of them, all nodding their heads, chanting a low sound. So strange. What's it all about? It's all so dark, but I don't know why?" Instinctively, Carita hears the worry in Humilia's voice and moves to calm her concern, yet there is in her questions the mystery that divides these Pilgrims from those she has grown up with, an almost palpable sour taste that comes with their arrogance and appearance of humility displayed in the street.

"It's their sacred season. They have to go to the hall to ask forgiveness. That's all I know. I didn't see them; I didn't go near Ypocrisis Street, I was late because of the gate."

So innocent, so simple. They know so little. Caught some how, not able to move forward. They're all like that. No drive. No desires. Just sit around talking. What kind of life is that? Shacks or ancient run down apartments to live in. No money ... no taste ... just get by, yet somehow content, even happy, before the occupation anyhow; now they live in a prison, guarded by those Pilgrims Carita saw. Oh, they walk to the hall alright; they should crawl they need so much forgiveness.

She doesn't know, doesn't know. People from everywhere, brought here to jump the population. Parasites, living off the money of others, grubby zealots that control the bureaucrats by stuffing their pockets. But why should I condemn them? Haven't I done the same? My whole career fed off these animals. I know them, I understand what Carita and Humilia could never know. I'm one of them. The worst.

What did she say? It struck me. Ah, 'it's all so dark.' Yes, it's all so dark. Darkness of belief that abandons all, save self. To be of the chosen ... that is darkness. Living alone in the doubt that festers in belief that can't be justified ... can't even be reasoned. Knowing every flaw that gnaws inside twisting innards like a knot, the cancer that kills certainty, the slow, silent toxin that

tells of the weaknesses that lacerate confidence ... all this must be hidden lest another know the faults. That's a prison worse than walls. That's my life. And I know where it began, the day, I know the day ...

As the months passed, fewer and fewer hospital personnel attended the Patient. He was moved from the VIP suite with its own entrance foyer, visitor's parlor, plush maroon leather chairs, and portraits of former heads of state to the third floor where he now rests with others in a care unit near the palliative ward where those without life support are made comfortable as they await death.

Humilia was assigned to day duty, a job that requires checking the monitors for his vital signs, replacing the fluids that keep him breathing, changing the sheets daily, and bathing the patient. Her position requires that she wear the nurses green over-garment, a loose fitting gown that leaves her maximum freedom of movement. She does not wear her hijab during the work day, only a small white nurse's crown that sits atop her coiled brown hair. She's been at this job for eight long months now, so long that the anticipated end of the coma has ceased to be an expectation. Yet for Humilia, the care of the Patient has become a sacred responsibility, especially as others abandoned his care.

For the Patient, the passage of time means little and the gradual abandonment by government officials, former military colleagues, religious leaders and family had no immediate impact. It took weeks before he understood how few came to see him, weeks during which he retained the belief that he was still in charge and return to his position was imminent. Once he realized, through a passing comment by a medical assistant, that he had been placed in the hands of an Elusian nurse and no longer attended to by the senior Nefarian hospital staff, he exploded inside with angry tirades against Humilia and her aide, Carita. But no one responded to his frustrations; his care had been placed in the hands of those he despised. From that day of awareness forward he could only confront his humiliation with vicious accusations to Humilia followed by contrition as he gradually understood that she, and she alone, cared for him.

Humilia trained in this hospital three years ago having arranged to live with her grandmother in her home in the old city where she has lived for sixty years; Humilia's parents live in Elusia, a territory that abuts Nefaria and is occupied by the Nefarian military.

Her grandmother's house is literally within the walls of the old city, its rooftop overlooks these walls to the east; but if one looks to the north, the most ancient Dijsam in the old city rises just beyond the electric wires, the barbed wire that scrolls over the stucco wall that surrounds the holy building, and the checkpoints that guard the entrance. Every day Humilia walks the same route home as she did this evening. She thinks frequently of her Patient, wondering what his life is like inside that immobile body.

'What if he can think,' she muses. 'What if he has listened and understood all these days. How would he respond if he could?"

But her thoughts are interrupted by the reality she walks through once beyond the check point at the gate. She shuffles slowly through the crowds that move in two directions through the narrow alley, the granite block walls rising on both sides punctuated by rust grated doors, green painted window frames covered with steel mesh, old and torn posters still pasted to the stained block walls, abandoned fruit cartons, black plastic garbage bags, loose papers, bits of wood strewn on the rising steps she must climb while avoiding the smooth stone inserts that enable a wheeled cart to traverse the steps, and the ever present surveillance camera above the gothic arch shrouded in shadows with pin points of light beyond. As she emerges from the shadows, an orange glow bathes the small plaza outside the Dijsam now crammed with twisted, stained green panels, huge cement buckets stuffed with brown sand bags, and small battered steel and canvas buildings that surround the guards now placed at the grounds. Above her head, electric wires and telephone lines, strung from the high walls to haphazardly placed poles, lace the face of the Dijsam like strokes of a black marker.

> "How ugly all this is," she mutters. "Barbed wire surrounding a Dijsam, ugly brown uniforms, guns; they just mock our faith – what do they care?"

A few steps beyond, she enters the narrow arched doorway into a gray slate foyer with two doorways to the left, entrances to two small apartments but home to large families, and a stairway to the right, a narrow, stone set of stairs that twists its way upward to a landing and the doorway to Nanya's home in the old city.

The door to her home is to the left, a small entrance with a glass window covered with a curtain. To the right, there's a small grotto area with a wooden bench and two chairs, a place of refuge against the summer sun, now abandoned to the cold.

Once inside, she removes her coat and scarf, calls to her grandmother, and goes to the kitchen. It's dark inside, only the evening light through the small window illuminates the kitchen. The ceilings are low, the rooms very small. The apartment is empty. She turns hurriedly to the door and goes outside.

"Nanya, Nanya!" she calls, but the wind silences her call.

She turns to the stairs that twist their way to the roof that is laced with clothes lines, and capped with vent pipes, TV antennas and rounded domes, the visible exteriors of vaulted ceilings that connect stairwells below.

"What are you doing on the roof, Nanya? It's past the curfew hour; it's dangerous up here. Everyone's supposed to be in an hour ago, and the soldiers are right across the street."

"Why are you home so early?"

"Because, Nanya, there was nothing more I could do for him. Nothing's changed. He lies so still. I can't even see his breathing without looking at the monitor. He might as well be dead."

"How can you not see him breathing? He's a big man, a huge belly, a fat face. I've seen him!"

"Be kind, Nanya, he's dying and we must be kind." Her voice is exceedingly tender to her grandmother for she knows her entire life has witnessed the transformation of Elusia and its people. Nanya knows from experience the futility of dreams.

"Forgive me, Humilia, I know we must forgive; but to know that youare responsible for caring for *this* man, this monster that crippled your father and caused such pain in your village, makes it hard to find forgiveness." There's pain in her words driven by the memory that destroyed the family's hopes in less than five minutes, forcing her to keep constant vigil over the anger and hate that festers inside, a cancerous tumor that ebbs and swells as the visibility of the NOF grows with each passing day.

The two stand on the rooftop above the small apartment. Nanya had pulled sheets from the clothes line and tossed them in a basket near her feet. Humilia crosses behind her grandmother, a small bent over figure garbed in a dark brown jilbaab, to remove the laden basket. Both stand quietly for a moment looking beyond the roofs to the distant hills that stand silhouetted against the sky. The sun slides quietly beyond the rooftops in the distance. There's a silence now. No one is in the streets and alleys below. There's no movement around the Dijsam. It is as it used to be, before the occupation, before the sirens, before the soldiers with their carbines and helmets, before life changed, in Elusia.

DAY ONE

Awareness

As she closes the door behind her, the cold morning wind whips at her face catching the folds of her head scarf pulling it open. She grabs at it just as she starts down the stairs. Once she enters the alley below, the wind stops, blocked by the buildings and wall. But the wind's wail cries above, sending an eerie sound echoing through the labyrinth of alleys and archways that snake through the old city. Humilia makes her way past the weathered green doors of the shops that line Despondah Street, still pad locked because of the curfew now in its fifth day.

She knows she must be careful; soldiers are on guard because of the curfew. She must walk deliberately or they'll think she's up to something. They can see so easily from where they are.

When she enters the open space in front of the Dijsam, she sees the military's netting covering their guns on the roof tops of homes that had once belonged to Elusians but are now homes for Nefarian Pilgrims. Here she looks up at the sky as the fall clouds race over head.

But once she enters the alley at the opposite end, the narrow space above her is covered with chicken wire netting filled with garbage tossed by the Pilgrims at the crowds below. The rotted fruit and meat casts a rancid smell over everything, caught as it is between the high walls of the homes and the corrugated tin that holds up the netting. The overcast sky allows little light through the twisted mesh where torn bags of garbage bulge through the holes above her head. As she arrives at the end of the street, she sees the check point ahead guarding the gate out of the old city. A line of people, shorter than usual because of the curfew, waits beneath the tin roofed cattle run, bordered on both sides by chain link fencing. She gets in line.

"Nothing changes," she muses, "Day after day we stand in line; leave early just to stand in line, it takes so long. For what? To pass through our own wall if we have their permission. What irony, I go to care for him month after month, their favorite son."

Once beyond the Elusian section, Humilia enters a different world. She now walks on swept sidewalks past renovated store fronts, windows filled with expensive clothing – wine-red, leather designer shoes, rich black boots trimmed with white fur, gray-green tweeds and deep blue pin-striped suits, lace blouses, pleated silk skirts, sunglasses of various shades in anticipation of the spring – others with intricately designed silver jewelry, red velvet lined cases of tableware, and ancient artifacts -- lures for the tourists that come to this holy city throughout the year, but especially now when the sacred days of forgiveness and retribution cast their shadow over all as the lunar year comes to its close.

The holy days serve as a year end shroud calling the laity to remember their sins, most importantly those that did harm to others, to publicly do penance by joining their fellows in pilgrimage to the many Assembly Halls that dot the city or to travel to their villages and walk with their townspeople to the hall there. Always before them stand the Divines who admonish the penitents of the punishment that befalls those who fail to forgive. Humilia knows little of these customs and ancient traditions; she is caught between two worlds, one she lives in every day that is itself split into two, the alleys she has just left and the street she now walks, the second in her spirit, where the teachings of her Ammars battle with the reality that presses down upon her.

The icons of the holy days adorn the flags that hang from street light poles, the banners that fly in the wind stretched between buildings, and the articles in store windows: everywhere the silver circle with the two arrow points facing each other, the visible signs of forgiveness and retribution, four candles attached to a circle representing the four seasons that mark the lives of those who must meditate on their past sins, and a circle set ablaze on its outer rim to remind all of the retribution that will follow. These days stretch on from mid-November through mid-December, days of remembrance, meditation, forgiveness, and fear. Music from loud speakers rides above the crowds that swarm through the streets, solemn, meditative laments befitting the sacred days. Despite the elegance of Ypocrisis Street with its high rise buildings clothed in blue glass, there is an aura of introspection that hovers in the air, a silent acceptance of human frailties that must be addressed, and judgments made.

It did not take long for Humilia to walk down these streets to the hospital that sits back from the road with an imposing entrance framed by two marble pillars crowned by a wrought iron arch capped by the seal of the state. She turns in at the gate and makes her way toward the side entrance knowing that she will have to show her permits and ID at the door. The magnificence of this building strikes her again as it always does; the white granite has been recently cleaned so that it shines in the sun.

"How beautiful that building is, so white and soft, like the snow that falls all about it. But I feel guilty liking it; so different from inside the wall where grime covers everything, even doors and windows have a sooty slime over them … and the garbage, the smells."

These thoughts carry Humilia around to the building's side entrance. She knows this place, she knows its purpose. The hospital provides state of the art care for government officials, the wealthy elite, and foreign dignitaries. Graduates of its renowned nursing school can find employment anywhere in the country, but many choose to stay here, especially those from Elusia, since no hospitals continue to operate in the occupied territory. Besides, there is need for some who speak Elusian to work at the hospital; that, in fact, played a role when Humilia was hired since many of the working staff did not speak Nefarian and she could serve as interpreter.

"Every morning I feel the same way when I open this door. I sense his presence as though he knows I'm here, yet nothing has changed. Nothing moves. Only the monitor's red line glows; he still breathes. How can he be alive and not know something, know I'm in the room with him. I can't help but feel he senses my presence. How strange to think he can hear me and say nothing, try to reach out even, to touch me. I feel like I'm caring for a ghost that understands but has been isolated from being in the world he knows, even worse, locked inside this body that everyone has abandoned. A pall of indifference hangs over this room. His own people have left him alone; no visitors, no family even. Only me, only one of the despised."

Unbeknownst to Humilia, the Patient senses her presence, perhaps because the door slid shut with a gentle click. He waits, as he has for months on end in timeless darkness, anticipating her arrival. She has become his lifeline, his tether to each day that gives reality to his now. He wants to hear her voice, the tremulous caring sound that greets him, announcing like some King's envoy, the passage of time. How different her coming is now from that first month and the second. How he hated the fact of her presence, her caring tone, her soft voice speaking to him, his dependency on an Elusian. But time, even unknown time, changes how the Patient feels towards this girl he does not know.

The morning sun's rays enter the window near the foot of the bed casting a soft glow over the taut sheets and the Patient's face. The sharp angles created by the sun's reflection appear like the chiseled form of a Gothic relief accentuating the stillness of his body. At the foot of the bed, his feet point stiffly upwards causing the sheets to flow gently over his form toward his chin. His marbleized face, lifted slightly on the raised pillow, gleams in the soft light making his fallen jowls smooth and round and his eyelids large and bulging. Humilia stands silently in the doorway looking at this immobile form before she removes her coat and scarf to begin the morning ritual of bathing and changing sheets. She notes the rise in the stomach area, the sunken chin, hooked nose and balding head. The sculpted form does not hide the short, stout, bulbous man that has dominated this nation's affairs since before she was born. As she moves closer, the soft light hardens as it reveals the incised lines around the eyes and mouth, the crevices beside the nose, and the dark blotches dotting the jowls and forehead.

"Oh, God," she utters aloud.

She feels a sudden repulsion for this man who lies so motionless, so dependent on her care, so totally oblivious of her existence. She fights these feelings. Her faith does not allow for hatred, even that which grows fetus like in the gut, impregnated there when she was but a child watching armed men strike her father across the head, drag him from the kitchen, and crush his knees while they cursed him and beat him unmercifully. From that day on her father has been a broken man, crippled and confined to a wheel chair, unable to care for the family, a silent image of the proud and confident father she once knew. That scene, shoved these many years into the deepest recesses of her mind, now rises often to her consciousness as she passes through the gates to hand her permits and ID to the soldiers.

But the Patient hears her exclamation, the frightened tone that breaks from her unexpectedly. He knows the feelings embedded in that sound, the fear mixed with hate, though he knows nothing about Humilia's past or what gave voice to that exclamation. Those two words, so vehemently expressed, force upon him memories long since buried, memories seared into his consciousness never to be forgotten, ever to be the prod to his hatred for Elusians, a never ending vengeance against those who resist.

Long ago, long before he rose to power in Nefaria, he waited at a checkpoint for his son returning home on the local bus from school, when he saw the bus explode in an inferno of flame and flying debris. Within seconds he had pushed aside the twisted metal and shards of glass to reach the boy and pull him from the rubble into his arms. "Oh, God!", "Oh, God!" he screamed at the heavens, his voice suffocated by hate for the Elusian bomber that, in one second, obliterated the blood of Demas, erasing his name from the face of the earth. He vowed then that he would lock these barbarians out of his life and find every way possible to drive them from Nefaria. That vow gave life to all his subsequent acts as he moved through the ranks in the Nefarian military by demonstrating a merciless, destructive force against his enemies.

That same anger and hatred drove Humilia's brother to join the resistance in Elusia. He now resides in the southern most crowded and heavily occupied area of Elusia. She remembers his last email, just six days ago, that he will be returning to Joyoa on the Day of Absolution. That's her day off and she hopes to go home also, but travel is so difficult with all the check points and the good roads closed to Elusians. She'll have to use the bus that cuts over the back hills, a shorter distance, yet a dangerous one if the soldiers move to intercept it. But she wants to see Ismaal so badly; it's been more than five years now since she has seen her brother, and she'd only have the one day. The day he left, her mother bundled some bread and water on the smallest donkey and left with him up into the mountains, the longest and most arduous route to southern Elusia. Two weeks passed before her mother returned. But, if Humilia is to see him, it must be on the Day of Absolution, four days from now, because she has to return to the Patient on the last day of the sacred season, the Day of Retribution.

DAY TWO

Humility

Awake again. How awake if I can't see or touch or talk to anyone? What is awake? My world's turned in on itself; I'm my world. Nothing else exists but my memories and what I hear at moments. How do these become real since neither is unless I want it to be …. Even then it has no meaning because no one knows what I think. I float in nothingness except this blackness … this absolute void of emptiness, without form; the day before creation … before anything was and nothing moved upon the face of the earth. I am nothingness lost in profundity … a contradiction … my sole purpose indulging self since I am who am. If I forget, I cease … all ceases.

Endless night. Formless, opaque … Time without sun, without stars even, without shadows, without clouds … 'the palpable obscure' that greeted Satan. Now me …

Beyond time I lie unknown and unknowing. Why? Why do I lie here weaving in and out of consciousness, tantalized by what I hear, taunted to hope beyond belief, to break from this coffin and let my mind wander over the earth that I can no longer see and fashion designs I would impose if I had the means ... Dragged, hung and quartered in this mind that is lashed by dreams and desires that exist isolated in a dead corpse ... What have I done to deserve such a fate?

What time is it? What day, what hour? What difference does it make? No sounds break my thoughts ... I lie here waiting, waiting for the unknown while others bustle around in their known world as though it alone gave them meaning; but how have they meaning if they do not know that life lies beside them and yearns to be recognized? Is life only what you know? Are lives lived in shadows, out of the glare of scrutiny, only specters without shape or being or purpose?

How many have I touched that I did not know and did not care to know? ... Are minds that think disposable because I do not know they are? Is reality my conception only, a commodity I can mold at my whim? Am I destined to lie here in this dark dungeon to contemplate the horrors I have wrought, to see what I never saw when I lumbered over the hills and valleys of this destitute land, to understand the meaning of the woe I have wreaked on this sad earth?

What irony is this ... to know what cannot be shared, to suffer a punishment no one can witness, to die each moment I wake. Why do these thoughts haunt me now? What changes wash over me in this silent tomb? My thoughts no longer rush to defend what I have done; I don't even feel the surge of hate that jumped in my gut when I saw an Elusian, the butchers of my boy. Their laziness, their filth, their smell no longer repels. Where's my vow now? Worthless scum, untouchables, for God's sake, yet Humilia enters so quietly, sings so softly, talks to me even though I lie here unable to move, to utter a word, to reach out, nothing but nothing. How I disdained this girl, how I hated the very thought that she would touch me, a Nefarian. Oh, if she had heard me then. But where are the others? Why only Humilia? Why?…. why? …why …

These thoughts plague the Patient moments before Humilia enters the room. By the time she closes the door, he has fallen into a deep sleep. Every day is the same; he wakes to hear sounds that break his slumber, and just as suddenly, he fades into unconsciousness. There is no continuity, no way for him to follow a conversation that lasts minutes or to meditate over time on an incident or thought that jumps to mind. He lives in a patch work world of bits and pieces, fragments of now and remembrances of time past.

Humilia and Carita bustle about the room that glows white in the florescent lights that bounce off the walls and reflect off the stainless steel counter tops and chairs. Everything shines. They throw the soiled sheets on the floor and kick them aside. While one holds his form up under the torso, the other shoves the clean sheets beneath him. Humilia wipes down his body with soft scented cloths as Carita takes the soiled linens to the laundry. They have established a routine by now, each knowing what the other must do. This day holds more expectation than most since they know a visiting neurosurgeon is scheduled to come to assess the Patient's progress and the procedures used to maintain his life.

"The doctors will be here in an hour or so; let's go to lunch. Where's your bag? I left mine in the closet."

"Mine's just outside the side door. I wanted it to stay cool, Humilia ... I hate soggy bread. I'm glad this is done for now. Let's go."

After picking up their lunches, they go downstairs to the Hospital cafeteria, a public area that serves a few hot meals and a variety of sandwiches, mostly for visitors and staff personnel. The line waiting to pick up trays extends into the hall. But they are not there to get food, only to find a table as far away from the crowds as they can get. This private time they cherish and, despite being on the staff, they know they are only tolerated, not accepted as equal. But alone they feel content and begin to talk in earnest.

Humilia returns to the question Carita asked when she first arrived in the morning, a question that Humilia felt had gone unanswered.

"You remember this morning when you asked about the Pilgrims and their walk to the Temple?"

"Yes, but it's not important. I was just curious; they seem so strange out there in the street."

"No, no, I do know a little bit," Humilia interrupts. "Fatima explained it to me last year. I don't remember all she said, but it's a yearly ritual." Humilia feels she knows something of the sacred season because she has lived in Desperia for the past three years, and, while marginalized by the Nefarians with whom she must work, her friends living near her Grandmother explain for her the strange behavior that she's been witness to in those parts of the city controlled by the Nefarians.

"It's supposed to be like the Christian pilgrims who make a spiritual journey to a sacred place to renew their commitment to Christ, but theirs is in the spring. Anyway, that's what Fatima told me and she's a Christian."

"What's the difference between commitment and forgiveness and retribution? I don't understand that," Carita's voice seemed to express an annoyance.

"Their pilgrimage is to seek forgiveness for what they have done in the past year; that's why it comes in the fall before the new lunar year. I don't think it's the same at all. The Christian's pilgrimage is in the spring and it's for renewal. These Pilgrims seek forgiveness from their God."

"But these are the people who attack us," Carita's voice reflects her anger. "They stopped my young sister on the way to school and called her names and threw tomatoes at her. She's only eight. They throw the garbage. Do they seek forgiveness for that?"

Humilia takes a drink from her water bottle before answering. "Well, if they do, I don't know who gives it to them. They didn't throw tomatoes at their God and they don't ask us."

"I guess not. That's why I'm confused. Now," Carita continues, "they're lined up on the street's edge, all dressed in black long-coats with something like a black khimar over their head and shoulders. They look like Knights Templar in the old books about the Crusades. Every one of them has a banner on a pole, a deep purplish-red color like the veins that run down my great grandmother's arms and hands, and all of these banners have the same image on them, a golden ring with two arrows pointed at each other. They appear very humble, but I can only think of what they did to my sister and old man Spea." A darkness comes over the conversation, imperceptibly, as the girls disclose to each other personal reactions to the Pilgrims who appear sinister, aloof, and dangerous.

"I don't know, Carita," Humilia responds thoughtfully, "it seems to me that they don't think they do anything wrong. Almost every family I know has had their kids taunted and hit. That's not the worst that they do by any means. Look what they did to my father and that was years ago. My cousins had their trees uprooted for the Wall they've built. Now they can't get to the fields that are left without going through a checkpoint."

"That's the same thing that happened to my brother and his family. And they just took his land, 'military security' they claimed. Just lies."

"Maybe they need forgiveness for not making our lives even worse," Humilia replies her voice dropping to a murmur as she utters this sardonic comment, though in its muted sound the corrosive tenor of its mockery is lost on Carita. A moment passes before Humilia mutters, "I don't understand."

"What is there to understand, Humilia? They took away the homes above Despondah Street, just came in one day with the army and told our people who lived there to get out. They had guns. There was nothing we could do. They go where they want, do what they want to us, shut down our shops, harass our children, destroy the fruit stands, mock the old shop keepers …

nobody can stop them with the soldiers all around." Carita's voice rises as she calls to mind the humiliation and pain she has witnessed. A few of the others eating in the cafeteria turn as Carita's agitation mounts. Humilia notices their expressions but fails to stop Carita who bursts out, "Listen! You remember old mister Spea, the tomato seller on Despondah Street, he's got the last stand before the square?"

"Quietly, Carita, they're looking at us."

"Oh, let them, maybe they'll learn something. Anyway, Old man Spea was sitting on a crate in the doorway last week, Friday, with tables covered with tomatoes outside the door, I was there, when a kid, a Pilgrim kid, maybe nine or so, came to his shop. He picked up a tomato and threw it at old man Spea, then another and another. No one standing around could believe what they saw, but they couldn't stop him, there were soldiers in the street watching this and they didn't do anything. Then he turned over one of the tables filled with tomatoes spilling them onto the street. The kid turned laughing and went down the street. Old man Spea just asked, just asked no one in particular, 'Who's going to teach him respect for elders?'

"All that is wrong," Carita says in frustration and anger, her voice swelling as she speaks, indeed, her whole body agitated, her eyes black and intense, her forehead creased, "You know that, I know it, everyone knows it. But nobody stops it. They don't walk down our streets asking for forgiveness; no chanting, no bobbing heads, no wailing tears of sorrow. Who do they ask for forgiveness? Beelzebub?"

"Carita, I don't know. I don't know their religion. It's strange. They seem to believe that they are above all other people, accountable to no one. I always thought religion brought people together so they helped each other. I thought it taught how to respect others and how to protect them against thieves and cheats and liars. But the Pilgrims do the opposite and no one seems to care. Why?" The conversation takes an unexpected turn as both girls respond to a deep anxiety and fear, feelings usually suppressed, even unacknowledged day to day, but which erupt when forced to confront the atmosphere that envelops their community and can strike without warning.

"Oh, Carita, I almost forgot, last night I spoke with Nanya about the Pilgrims. She started to cry, without my saying anything but the name; she buried her face in the edge of her khimar. But then, after a while, she told me about that morning when they beat my father, and then went on about other times when they came into Desperia, right to her door. All of them wore masks and carried steel rods. They broke the window on her door, shouted curses, and threatened her. She had fled the room to hide in a closet."

"Why would they do that? She's a little old lady; she can't hurt them." Carita leans forward touching Humilia's hands in sympathy.

"I'm getting to that," Humilia continues, "they broke dishes, turned plants upside down and left. Later Nanya found out from others in Despondah Street that they had smashed down doors just to frighten everyone, make them want to leave. That's what they want, make us leave so they can take more of the houses."

"That's so horrible."

"She also told me a strange thing from years ago when she was in Joyoa. Pilgrims spread turquoise pellets on the hills where the sheep grazed, poison pellets, so sheep would die and no one would know why. When she talks like that, I feel so helpless. Why can't something be done? Where are our neighbors? Why don't they help? Where are the great countries that talk of liberty and freedom for everyone? Why does no one care? Tell me."

But neither Humilia nor Carita wait for an answer. They gather the stained paper that covered the sandwiches, the water bottles, and the bags, and move to the exit. They must be at their station before the doctor comes with his attendants.

****

Many doctors watch over the Patient. His care has been mandated by the ruling party. Even in this condition, no one dares malign this man. But the impending arrival of the neurosurgeon lifts concerns for his condition to another level. What prognosis might emerge that would hint at possible recovery? What chance exists, in this nebulous world of medical predictions, that he could return to a full functioning state? So much hangs in the balance, so many lives affected, so many unknowns that would upset what had been put into place since he entered the coma.

An entourage approaches his rooms from the central stairway, some in military uniforms, others in pin striped suits, and the doctor, garbed now in his blue surgeon's gown. Humilia and Carita stare at this imposing group. They had forgotten how important their patient is to the Nefarians, it's been so long since anyone, even doctors, came to see him. But here they are. A gaggle of sounds accompanies their arrival. Yet one voice stands out from the rest, perhaps in deference to his status as the neurosurgeon, perhaps because he commands authority with the force and curtness of his commands. All seem to be attentive as he directs them to places around the Patient's bed. He then proceeds to lecture the group, or it appears to Humilia that he is lecturing because when she turns toward that voice she realizes he is speaking without ever having examined her Patient.

What voice is that? Ah, I know ... 'Hey, Fatstuff, get on your knees for me. C'mon you Butterball ... beg for me, yeah.' ... God, that voice ... the sound stirs ... what? ...I know! ... Dear God ... that high pitch, that scowl, that bastard from the academy ... What are you doing here? What nightmare plagues me. ... Oh, God, you're over me ... you monster. What fate brings you here when I'm castrated ... no voice, no sight, no power to hurl at you, you Apollyon! I'm just an immobile hulk at the mercy of any who stare or smirk or sneer at my empty shell. What humiliation! My bulbous dead face, blotched skin, a thing to ridicule and scorn ... helpless, so helpless.

Are you mocking me now, you bastard? Are you having fun, calling me 'butterball,' 'fatstuff,' 'puffball,' the ignominious curses of the privileged that scars even now ... the country bumpkin. I was ripe for your derision and disdain. You drove your verbal knives deep; you made me hate myself, made me long for revenge ... to cut you to the quick, to see you cry, squirm, run from me ... but it will never be.

You played with me, the fool waiting alone, always waiting but never chosen, stole my clothes when I was in the shower, hid my food, laughed when I couldn't answer a question. Butterball the icon of stupidity, the minstrel's fool, last at the table, a buffoon to make others laugh, a caricature, despised, mimicked, the butt of clowns.

I hate you. Such irony now ... hate inside a mute helpless form. The last ignominy you thrust at me – haul me naked from the shower, stuff me inside the locker ... Laughter rings outside my metal cage, taunts and jeers, the ringing clang of fists and bottles against the steel lockers thunders in my ears ... I weep, and through my tears I look out, through the slits, at the bent over laughing bodies of the students, their faces twisting into the sinister sneers of gargoyles. All ... all laughing at me ... the caged fat monkey ... a figure of shame, a submissive nothing ... the stamped image of savage servility.

I vow ... never ... never. I vow to myself ... I curse the God that made me ... I believe in that curse ... I will never submit to any man. No man will have my respect. I will cloak my scorn for all beneath the smile that holds back my mockery ... I will walk this barren earth a seething cauldron of hate, subject to none, obedient only to my ambition and anger, the twin engines of my means to power ... Such has been my life from that hour.

As Humilia stands listening to the surgeon, as the minutes pass, she feels her innards tense; a deep sense of unease comes over her. She backs towards the door hoping to escape the pressure that surrounds her. She feels the Patient's helplessness and knows he longs to be free. Nothing she feels makes sense. Where does this agony come from; what connection ties these two and her to him?

"Nurse, Nurse, where are you going? I'll need your charts, don't leave here, you hear me?"

"Yes, I hear you, sir, but I thought you didn't need me since you began your evaluation without needing those charts."

"Don't question my authority, young lady. I'll tell you when you can go. Do you understand?"

"Yes, sir."

Humilia reacts instinctively, speaking for her Patient, in an unexplainable symbiosis with him, a man she had never seen before or spoke with. She knows and feels in her soul the destructive nature of this doctor that somehow formed the character of the patient she cares for, now defenseless and alienated in the very world he designed and forced into being.

Humilia does not understand her feelings; she knows only the pity that stabs at her for her Patient in the presence of this doctor. Something in her gut reacts to his sinister, arrogant, self-absorbed manner. She knows, he knows no one else. The world exists for him alone. He stands there spouting to these lapdogs, and they smile at him as though their lives depend on his acceptance of their doting. None of them would willingly give him the time of day had they a chance to survive without his say so. She longs to be at home, to be with those she loves, to serve them tea, to joke and laugh in kindness. How revolting this driven world of the Pilgrims and Nefarians who climb over each other to get ahead.

Humilia intuitively senses the connection between the doctor and her Patient. Something in his tone, its strident, absolute ring that hints of scorn and disdain, signals to her that he feels victorious over this prone and defeated figure. He has not come to heal; he's come to gloat over this man that has ruled this country for so long, a man he has despised and envied since they went to school together before he entered medical school and his nemesis the military. Their lives moved in different circles though each knew of the other, even followed in secret his career, perhaps even longed for a reunion in hopes that somehow he could publicly humiliate his enemy.

Ah, Humilia, you stand in the shadow of evil personified. But you, my innocent, know it not. What courage to stand up to him, a mere nurse from Elusia … not courage, what do you know of courage? … It's character. It's you … how you sense people, know goodness, see evil cloaked in a blue doctor's gown. You respect the person, not his gown or his title. An ass is an ass no matter the dress …Ha! Garb the pig in cape and crown and it still smells. … You know and do not bow. Nefarians bow. God damn, they crawl if they must. Success demands it. Not in Elusia. Your happiness is in the home not the business. Enjoying each other not trampling each other. It's a way I've never understood. Hell, I hated it, I mocked it. I mocked you for leaving your Joyoa to attend me. What fun … I was one of the soldiers, one of the beasts that crippled your father! Crippled him? I showed the Pilgrims

how to do it. How fitting the insult, and you don't even know who you care for or what I did to your family. Would you be so nice if you knew?

Now ... now in this silent morgue I sense what I never thought to consider before -- my arrogance is my albatross. I know the character of Nefarians, I know what goads them, what fear drives their ambition, what self doubt serves as quicksand of superiority, what weight, in centuries of suffering and violence, they bear ... carrying their forebears on their backs, the pain and guilt of centuries. ... what vengeance churns inside the soul, what inferiority forces them to destroy and bury any guilt or shame. This I know and use because I am Nefarian. I've been deluged with the fear that grips a people who have been maligned, mauled and murdered, driven from country to country, detested by all, and I know what it does to the soul ... vengeance conquers mercy, ruthlessness rides roughshod over pity. But I don't know the Elusians. I thought I did; in my arrogance I thought I did.

"I need those charts now, Nurse. Quickly, quickly, we haven't much time. These are important people; we can't keep them waiting, they've things to do."

Humilia hands the charts to the doctor with an obvious disdain, one he recognizes but to which he cannot now respond. He ushers the entourage to an adjacent room where numerous computers flank the far wall. He sits on a wheeled stool and rolls before the screen.

"Let me show you the most recent cat scan of his skull; it demonstrates my point. This is a top down image. Note the white areas on the interior side of the skull ... the blood. That creates pressure against the brain itself. It also prevents normal motor movement. The brain no longer functions to control impulses that guide motion. This is a severe case. No motion at all. He's been reduced to a breathing specimen without sense reaction of any kind. There's no reason to keep him alive except in deference to his former status. A waste of money and valuable man hours really. But, then, it's not my call. Politicians have to earn their keep."

With that brief summary, the doctor rises from the stool, and perfunctorily asks the assembled if they have any questions, knowing from his manner that they would not deign to ask. He bows ever so slightly and exits the room handing Humilia the set of charts as he leaves. He never glanced at them.

The doctor's marked indifference to his supine patient, indeed, his abhorrence and disgust at having to appear concerned, reflects an arrogance that dominates the professional class in Nefaria. Ironically it is the same trait that characterizes the Patient. Neither man has any respect whatsoever for the darkly clad Pilgrims that walk the streets and publicly display their penance, yet neither man would outwardly show his contempt because, quite frankly, each has manipulated the Pilgrim's superstitions to his advantage.

Deep inside these men rests an absolute conviction that they are innately superior to the masses, not because their religion teaches such superiority, for neither believes in the religion of their fathers, but because they believe in an inherent superiority for some necessitating a class that must reign superior to the masses. Both accept the necessity of a ruling class even if that rule is imposed by force, stability requires it. To that end, use of groups, especially religions, becomes a natural part of the ruling process. Such convictions give license to control by cunning and force, by those arrogant enough to assume power to themselves and forget the prophets of old that warned of impending doom.

DAY THREE

Contrition

After the departure of the doctor followed by Humilia and Carita, their work day now done, the Patient lies still, oblivious to all that ensued after he fell into sleep or unconsciousness. As night falls, the bright lights throughout the hospital are turned down. Only dim hall lights glow through the windows and a gradual calmness suffuses all. It is as though no life breathes; rather a stillness, a silence pervades the air waiting for some anticipated yet unknown presence to enter. Time passes peacefully around the lifeless figure as the dim dawn of a new day emerges. How strange that, in this apparent peacefulness, a mind wakes grasping to hold onto consciousness, alone in his black world, his mind tottering on an abyss of nothingness.

I am the way into the woe of everlasting torment. Dante himself could not design my fate. Who could contemplate a time without end filled with self inflicted

punishment for every treacherous act against neighbor or deceit against friends, even kin? ... "Abandon all hope ye who enter here," Dante carved above the portal of Hell. But he did not enter his own hell. He suffered only the pain that greets the suffering of others, and that only because he had a conscience. I face myself, not the face of deceit, but the mind that designed it. It's my hell, a hell I can't escape. ... I have no life but thought, a rampaging memory that propels me through this dungeon of despair and lashes my naked soul without mercy.

Why this torment? I believe in nothing but my own needs, my pleasures, my ambition. No God judges me. No hell awaits my entry. No fear of eternal damnation turns me into a driveling idiot. I scorn such weakness, the slobbering superstition of mindless fools. ... What then turns my thoughts into thorns that thrust themselves into my black night like the edge of daggers deep into this restless mind that cannot find peace?

Am I to understand now that I did not, could not control my fate? Does some residue of connection tie this bulbous buffoon to those he despised despite every desire to drain away all feeling? Do I face some malicious God who sits silently listening and laughing to my wayward thoughts? ... Has he designed this infernal tomb that surrounds me with absolute darkness the better to force me to confront my own thoughts, the only torture left to me? Am I to look back, remember every atrocity, judge myself?

Even now that massacre looms in this dark gloom. It's never far away yet it happened so long ago, fifty years ago at least. I watched them ... oh, why kid myself, I ordered them to slaughter those innocents ... just women and children locked in a refugee camp that I surrounded with tanks so none could escape. I looked into their lust filled eyes as they grabbed a girl, raped her, and shoved her to the next soldier. Such brutality I had never seen before. But I was worse ... I exulted in this savagery, I reveled in it. Why? Who am I to bathe myself in blood, listen with glee to dying screams, laugh at a baby's cry? I never let myself think like this ... no time to worry, to feel shame, just force, ruthless force. Is this my final destiny? Am I to spend this unending blackness wrapped in contrition, caught in the vengeance of a malicious God?

Then so be it. I have no Virgil to lead me into this unknown. ... So, Demas, let us go then, you and I, to meet the demons we will meet, bare our souls, for we have nothing to fear; there is no exit from here. I will to be to ...

But the Patient does not control his consciousness. Sudden lapses seize his mind and all goes silent. Yet, in those moments when he's alert, when voices penetrate his darkness, he responds in anger or despair, the spontaneous reaction to helplessness. Now, however, after all these months of isolation and suffering, he enters defiantly that last journey, the dark night of the soul. The Patient in his body, the room he lies in, the hospital itself, the resurrected old city of Desperia seem rooted in time, cradled graves that mirror human consciousness locked out of sight, buried perception lost forever, never to slither imperceptibly from its dank cellar into the light.

Desperia, an ancient city of vast treasures stretching back thousands of years, would seem to contain the dreams of humankind in its great seal, a lamp of learning set as a crown on a human skull. From that past comes knowledge and understanding to be discerned or discarded by those who seek.

****

On a map, Nefaria appears a splinter in the extended thumb of a curled fist, surrounded on three sides by neighboring nations and to the west the sea. It's a land of rolling hills and valleys covered with sand and rock, home to ancient civilizations whose existence lies buried beneath the barren, wind swept landscape. Intense heat pours down on the people in summer, and harsh cold winds carrying snow and hail blast the land in winter. Despite the extreme weather, peoples have lived here for millennia, alternately slaughtering each other or living quietly together in contentment if not peace.

Much of the slaughter has been inflicted by foreign nations that have colonized the land because it sits on the edge of other nations that have been subdued and occupied. Desperia reflects the history of Nefaria; its ancient walled city has been home to diverse peoples with different languages and customs, and they too have fought each other over the centuries. The great prophet Thorthana once observed that Desperia mirrors the great blue globe traveling alone through the heavens, viewed from afar it appears magnificent in its oneness, viewed up close, a shattered multi-colored looking glass of dreams deferred and justice denied.

The current state of Nefaria resulted from the colonial debacle that left the country severed into two parts dividing the population by ethnic roots. The Elusians, two thirds of the original population, did not accept the division imposed on them, and, as a consequence, lost all but a fragment of their original land to the militarily superior Nefarians. The occupation of Elusia continues to the present day.

For this reason the presence of the Pilgrims in such numbers and in such public display in Desperia creates tension within the Elusian people who live and work in the old city. Their public presence during the third day of the sacred season, the Day of Contrition, takes on an intrusive character as they stand in huddled groups on street corners up and down Ypocrisis Street which flaunts their sins in the circle of four candle flames on a scarlet flag flying from every lamp post, their black forms bent in prayerful somberness, bowing low and whispering acts of contrition drawn from the prophecies in the *Book of Judgment*. Aware as they are of the retribution to follow those who ignore the Days of Confession and Penance, they send forth a mournful dirge of sorrow for wrongs done,

"Hear now the trumpet sound that rings above the tempest,

Summoning to attention this assembled host;

Fear spreads as a darkened cloud over all this tribe

Who await the doom the Almighty might prescribe."

This dirge hums above the sound of cars and trucks caught as it is beneath the heavy clouds that hang over the city during this season of sin acknowledged and punishment feared. Stranger still are the blatant images of ancient sins displayed on enormous billboards attached to buildings, near naked women lounging on beach towels smoothing lotion on their legs, rollicking women and men drinking, and pornographic magazines touting sex. But for Elusians like Humilia and Carita, the apparent contrition appears to mask the reality of their deeds and mocks the very season that they display for the world to see.

The people of Elusia, unlike the Nefarian population, live meager, destitute lives, powerless to affect change since poverty envelopes the country and their very existence depends on the whim of the occupying force. No one can move in Elusia without the approval of the NOF which controls hundreds of check points throughout the land; no one can enter Elusia without the expressed permission of the NOF; no one can leave her house without an ID, no one can drive his car without the identifying license plate, and no one can travel the new roads designed for the Pilgrims who live in the Elusian areas in new developments protected by the NOF. Life in Elusia slides ineluctably into a hopeless passivity of alienation, despair and, all too frequently, a deep rooted hatred for their oppressors that explodes from time to time in ignominious acts of barbarism.

The Nefarian faithful finds solace in the intensity of their ritual and centuries of adherence to ancient beliefs. Precedent and tradition continue to unify the people regardless of historical change and scientific progress. The reestablishment of its homeland in Elusia has the authority of the blessed prophets who predicted the Nefarians' return to the covenanted land centuries ago.

The Elusian people find themselves ancestors to those subdued and conquered in all past civilizations, those enslaved and forced to relinquish their rights to the oppressor. While victims in fact, they are known by the Nefarians as a force that threatens the very existence of Nefaria, a belief fostered by the state to instill fear and compliance with authority. Hence Nefarian religious authorities, particularly the Divines, never fail to seize an opportunity to instill the ineluctability of prophetic power into the faithful including visits to the man most responsible for Nefaria's rise to power in the present, General Demas. At this very moment the good Divine Evangile has gathered a small group of Pilgrims at the bedside of the Patient.

"Quietly now, I need all of you to gather around the bed, not too close, a respectful distance please."

Divine Evangile admonishes his small group that had come to pray for the Patient. About twelve Pilgrims cloaked in black draw close to the bed, their heads bowed, beards resting on their chest, each nodding silently, with their prayer books pressed to their stomachs.

"As you know, our Leader has been in this coma thirteen months now. Few expect him to recover though there are those who know that he has before been left for dead on the field of battle only to return and lead his troops to victory. He is a strong and determined man. No man in our recent history has demonstrated more loyalty to our cause -- the return of our country to its rightful owners. He leads by example. He embodies our beliefs. He knows what resoluteness must be imposed on the Elusians if we are to succeed. And he knows that the world must understand that we do not wish harm to anyone. We desire more than all else peace. We are by nature peaceful people; we wish only to bring our wisdom and our morally superior way of living to this part of the world. It's our mandate from our prophets. We are only the willing and humble servants of our God. This man is our most sacred asset. We must pray for his recovery.

"Let us all remember how he brought us to this promised land and made possible the return of the sacred season of forgiveness and retribution. We owe him a debt of gratitude. Pray in your hearts for his soul that his sins be forgiven and that he suffer no retribution. He has given so much for this country. Please pray silently. We'll leave momentarily."

The Council of Ecclesiastic Divines proclaimed this year's sacred season to be of unusual significance precisely because the General that inaugurated the season as one of special meaning to the Nefarians, in light of the Prophet's signaling the days of judgment as imminent, lies stricken at the very moment of Nefaria's prophesied return to its ancient lands under the covenant. The Almighty must have known the convergence of these two events and hence the proclamation of this season as fulfillment of the prophecy through the efforts of this great man. Their merging of the sacred prophecies with the secular and military control of the Elusian land gives justification and credibility to the expansion even as it dwarfs the legitimacy of the Elusian claims.

Such fools. You come to pray for me. How ridiculous. Pray to a God that our forefathers created to control their people centuries ago. ... What a coup. Make you believe so the few can rule. Things don't change. Lemmings and leaders; it's always been so. The ruthless rule; fools follow. I learned that early; old Apollyon taught me well. Make God love the sheep, care for them in spirit, then let them be used. And all need only believe that there is a reward for suffering. Even now in this so called modern age, you crawl before this mirage. ...

Pilgrims, you are my creation ... fodder to feed my scheme to confiscate more land, always how to steal more land, and you never knew. ... God in heaven! ... you take my design and enlarge on it. You bring a fanaticism I had not known existed, a belief that blots out time, logic, even law ... No need, you claim, to legalize taking our land back ... God promised it by covenant thousands of years ago. I simply build on your zealotry. Intimidation and force... don't fight by the book ... surprise, impulsiveness ... that conquers all.

You driven lunatics live in my creation ... the colonies. I house you on Elusian land ... I give you guaranteed bargains ... all you must do is attack the Elusians -- burn their crops, dig up their fields, bulldoze their orchards and homes, make life impossible so they will leave.

I knew the Elusians would fight back and make peace impossible. I am the new king enticing the people to accept the inevitable will of God Almighty, citing their ancient prophets as irreconcilable truth ... I only need to guide the process. Now, I lie here numbed to life, unable to tell you how I have used you ... but why even think this ... I would never reveal any such thing. You are human collateral to make possible my Nefaria. I don't care any more for you than I do the Elusians ... besides, you have the season of forgiveness and retribution to cleanse the zealotry that drives your inhumanity ... I forged that season from ancient manuscripts to mold your beliefs ... and your obedience drives my political need. That deceit confirms for me that the seal of God's "chosen" assures blind obedience and absolute success ... Necessity drives ambition.

They're gone ... Only silence, the blackness of a cave. I'm alone again. ... I think differently when I'm alone. ... Something surges in my soul when I hear old enemies or idiots I've used ... or Humilia. They propel where my mind goes ... I luxuriate in defense of what I've done, it's so easy to savage fools and the innocent. ... But, when silence comes, when I must face myself, when the delight of inflicting defeat has retreated ... then this monstrous demon of doubt intrudes to destroy my certainty ... a certainty built to defend the savagery I leveled at the Elusians who, like all who fell in times past under the boot of the conqueror, must die ... yet now I crumble before this demonic force that I have buried for seventy years, my whole biblical age lived beyond the pale of damnation now haunts me. ... for I am alone -- judge, jury, and sole witness to this excruciating suffering, this torment that tears at me from this burial vault of decaying flesh. ...

The departure of the Pilgrims leaves the halls of the hospital quiet, and slowly the entire building becomes as silent as the Patient's tomb. Night to him exists only in its soundlessness, long passages of time without intrusion to stimulate his mind, often awake but unresponsive without a voice, a siren, or a distant explosion. To these he impulsively responds. They become catapults to past actions or decisions that he created and consequences he caused.

He brought the Sacred Season of Forgiveness and Retribution into existence with the help of the Divines and their Council of Antiquities. The season ignites a religious fervor that gives the Divines direct authority in the day to day life of the Pilgrims. It holds the threat of retribution before all including those who might disdain the power of the state's ministry. He grew in stature before the religious powers since he sought its resurrection from the prophecies of Thorthona, a prophet that lived over 3500 years ago. The Thorthana prophecies are existentially meaningful to Nefarians since they proclaim fulfillment in the present, in undetermined years at the beginning of this century. That fear of ultimate retribution serves the ends of both the state religion and the government.

The Thorthana prophecies exist in a tattered papyrus codex accidentally discovered 60 years ago. Because the prophecy plays an important role in this Patient's life, it is provided here so that all will understand its significance.

THE BOOK of JUDGMENT

By the Prophet Thorthana

In those days none knew the judgment of the Almighty Lord of the Heavens, though they knew His wrath and feared His unyielding retribution. None knew on what bedrock of justice the Almighty's Hall of Judgment stood nor in what hour He would call the Day of Judgment. Yet all knew that day would come. Now let all who would hear and understand listen to the prophecy of Thorthana for he has the voice of the Almighty Lord and sees what is yet to be:

As I lay a sleeping I saw God's wrath unfold,

A hideous vision, terrible to behold,

Of horrors that befell the vicious hounds of war

For crimes against their kind justice could not ignore.

I saw them all assembled before the golden throne,

Their numbed faces filled with fear for a fate yet unknown;

Around them swelled a sorrowful dirge, their mourning song,

A wail so sad, I wept for this pitiful throng.

But pity they did not deserve, I was to learn,

For in their greed filled lives they had chosen to spurn

The cardinal rule that gives life that all may live,

Learn to love all, so that all may learn to forgive.

Then before my eyes I saw a scene so profound,

I stood with those assembled, silent and spellbound,

As far above a silver bird hurtled through the sky,

Shattering the brilliant blue with its awful cry.

No sooner had that scream reached our ears when we saw

A burst of crimson flames break the blue and billow

Forth, as from a furnace set by some fiend unknown

To challenge the Almighty who sits upon His throne.

Then, without warning, the sky fell in molten ash

From its dome, blocking the morning sun, to crash

In peppered foam below, and cast an eerie pall

On all who walked, shrouding them in a ghastly shawl.

This dark scene intensified, as it unfurled

In a muffled silence so complete, it swirled

In eddies about the shadowed and muted feet,

Leaving a morbid tableau that death might greet.

But, then, a trumpet sound rang above the tempest,

Summoning to attention the assembled host;

Fear spread as a darkened cloud over all the tribe

Awaiting the doom the Almighty might prescribe.

****

This Day of Judgment I describe will transpire,

In due time before three millennium shall expire.

And all those living then shall know vengeance to fear,

That our inhumane acts become the sins all will hear.

Those who stand for judgment here have in life thwarted,

By deeds unbelievable, what reason intended,

While witness to their infamy stand those who died,

Cursed victims of wanton slaughter by those who lied.

****

The remaining portions of the manuscript are severely damaged and, while they seem to be a continuation of the prophecy, they cannot be rendered in the verse form adaptable to the beginning.

Suddenly I stood alone, invisible in the vastness of space,

The felt presence of Retribution's power hovering

In the canopy of the night sky like some impending doom,

A pall of unending shame that must descend on this place

And those who without remorse slaughter their kin.

Then did I know that I must record what Retribution would sow

In the minds and souls of those treacherous in life to their own

That they might know the fullness of Damnation's wrath.

As I trembled beneath that black canopy

Studded with pinpoints of light beyond number,

I heard a terrifying roar overhead

As the canopy rolled in rivulets from east to west,

A pulsating wave of raven hues bearing down upon the earth.

Then the Almighty's sword sliced through the canopy

Pouring the brilliance of the sun's white light

Onto the darkened hills below.

I heard the voices of Judgment ring

From out the brilliance of that light.

There I stood, witness to the Day of Judgment,

As the terrorists of humankind, in those days yet to come,

Faced the wrath of righteous retribution

To enter an eternity of unending punishment.

Moving slowly from the edge of darkness in the far off hills,

Forlorn groups of men moved inexorably to their doom.

The sun's light cut through the blackness to expose

A desert of white sand where those to be damned

Would hear their sentence while their victims swarmed

About them thick as locusts listening to the peals of thunder

That voiced their crimes and their punishment.

Out of that mass of loathsome men, shrouded in darkness,

Emerged a phalanx of horrid creatures moaning in anguish

As they moved inexorably into the light of recognition.

There they stood, a swaying mass draped in slime,
A putrefying mucus covering them, head to foot,

An apt cerecloth to wrap those doomed to eternal damnation.

Out of that moving mass rose a muffled lamentation

Of blurred sound like the never ending roar

Of the limitless sea, an appalling curse for all eternity.

This prophecy acts as the catalyst for the seven days of the sacred season; it serves to compel compliance before the imminent and vengeful wrath of the Almighty.

DAY FOUR

Confession

When Humilia arrives early at the hospital in the blistering cold, she notices the phalanx of military vehicles that circle the crescent drive before the main entrance with its fluted pillars and cornices. She senses that numerous officials must be visiting the bedside of her Patient, important officials since soldiers stand at attention beside each vehicle and two others at the doors. This will make it difficult for her and Carita to do their regular chores or force them to be postponed. That disturbs her. His care seems paramount in her eyes, after all, he is at death's door and his last days should be sacred. But those that do come to see him   do not show any concern for his condition other than a necessary obeisance to his former status. During her eight months in this position, Humilia has had to listen to the feigned praise of some, the obsequious eulogizing of others, and the virulent hatred of known enemies. Before she enters the side door, she knows the day will be a silent and ominous one.

Surrounding the Patient's bed stand five figures, two foreigners dressed in pin striped suits and three military, high ranking officers with full dress medals and epaulets. Humilia moves to the monitors with her record board, marks the figures, then returns to her station on the north side of the room. She does not dare intrude herself between the Patient and the visitors.

"He's been in this state for months now. No change." The speaker wears the uniform of the Nefarian Air Force with its distinctive deep blue jacket and light blue trousers with the gold stripe. He's tall and lanky with peppered hair and mustache. His billed hat fits comfortably under his left arm. "They've tried everything including cutting into the skull to allow for drainage of the excess blood. Nothing works. He might as well be dead. Yet he has such a following it behooves the administration to keep him on life support." The voice is authoritative and direct.

"But is there any expectation that he might come out of the coma? I'd like to be able to return home and present a full report to the Emperor." These words, uttered by the United Corporate States' Ambassador, a short, paunchy gentleman with a bald head, are offered hesitatingly and with a tone of decided concern.

"No one knows. And if he did, what condition would his mind be in? What control of his arms and legs would he have? I'll be blunt. The nation needs to get on with life after the General. He's had his day; we're in the next Nefarian period and the people need to accept that."

"I understand your point, Sir, but my country has invested heavily in this man. He in many ways 'is' Nefaria to my Emperor. He's been given free reign to run things here as he desired. We kept hands off even though there are many at home that claim he is the cause of terror hurled at UCS. Your country's policies against the Elusians causes hatred of us. But we haven't told our people what he's been doing, so they look to his condition and hope it will change."

"Let me butt in here, Mr. Ambassador." This blunt officer served with the Patient for many years in engagements in northern Nefaria and in incursions against neighboring states. Yet he suffers the ridicule of the Patient by being called a "wagon driver" because he wanted to warn civilians of impending action, something Demas scorned. "Why do your people not know what a bastard this man is? It's been open news in Nafaria for 50 years. He's driven by power; he must be in command. No principles guide him, just a ruthless retributive mission of destroying houses, killing dozens of women, children, and the elderly if it will secure his advancement. He equivocates, lies, and condemns those who oppose him."

"Should your brief bio become public knowledge in my country, the funding of Nefaria would stop immediately and the influence of the UCSNSA would cease to exist."

"The Nefarian Support Association in your country is run by fanatics that have vested interests in forcing your legislators to acquiesce to their demands. God, man, they write your legislation; they own you."

"That is not news to me, Sir. Nevertheless, they are the ones that crafted the UCS position and made him such an icon in our Congress. For you to turn him into a devil will not fly well with the Emperor."

This exchange between the foreign dignitaries and the officers takes place over the Patient's bed. Humilia weeps quietly in the background. She knows the Patient's spirit weeps with her as these insults and malicious accusations fly in the air. Yet she is powerless to stop it.

I lie? What do you think I should do when idiots make military plans that are doomed to fail? Yeah, Phala, General in name only, you fool. Why do you run from killing? That's war … I kill … I kill women and children if need be … now doesn't count, the future counts and if it's possible to control the future by killing than so be it. I write the news, God damn it, I make the news, I make Nefaria while you sit on your ass and cry. Go, get out of here you coward … if killing women and children bothers you, get a desk job. What makes you shrink from what has to be done?

This violent and scornful outburst against his fellow officers erupts from his silent crypt and casts him back into a dream like vision of his defiance years ago. He had received orders to clear out a village and then demolish the homes. A week after this alleged battle, newspapers reported the massacre of civilians found buried beneath the demolished homes. The Patient was brought before a board of supervisors to explain what had happened. In his vision he relives that day.

The bastards! ... What do they want of me? I haven't time to muck around, play nice cop to these vermin. I'm supposed to escort them out of town? ... Where should I put them? Who'll guard them? No, you chicken hawk idiots ... I'm in command ... I'll make an example of this town ... spread out, I don't care what the men do ... fuck the women, cut them open ... savage the children, the old men. Yell, 'Anybody home?' ... then throw the grenade, blow it up, don't wait for a response. I'll head the parade of carts that carry the bloody bodies stacked on each other like pig carcasses, legs spread to show what we've done. From town to town we'll show the bastards what happens to those who resist. Let the blood run like a river. The whole of Gallaria will be ours ... We'll tell the politicians what they want to hear. The town's been cleared ... that's all they need to know. It's all for Nefaria ... security for Nefaria ... It's justified ... Who cares what the outside thinks. They won't be able to stop us once the village is ours ... God in heaven, they won't know there's been a village. I bury villages ... bury the people in the rubble of their own home ... drive the rest away. It's what has to be done.

His mind revisits the past, reclaims the decisions he made, finds justification for his actions and mockery for those who opposed him. And his mind has churned these thoughts over and over and continues to churn them as day follows day and night follows night, a passage timeless to him as the months pass.

Phala, you coward, I had more courage when I was a raw cadet in the youth corps than you have now. God Almighty, I was made an instructor there before I was 15. Where were you? When did you put your life on the line for Nefaria. I did before it was Nefaria, just a dream in the heads of our founders. But I knew even then what had to be done, what ruthlessness had to be forced on the vermin that crawled around in our land. God, Phala, I was so good, even at that age, I could join a rogue unit of the terrorists to plague the Elusians and cleanse them from our land ... cleanse them? We drove them out by sheer force. That's what power's all about, you idiot.

There's no compromise. No sympathy for anyone. No kindness for the innocent. There's no innocence if you're against Nefaria. I remember the night we blew up the hotel ... not any hotel, but one holding a wedding crowded with guests, a hotel owned by the foreigners that controlled our lands before we drove them out. There were some Nefarians staying there, but that didn't matter. The enormity of the outrage, the sheer guts needed to destroy such a place ... that makes headlines. That causes things to change. Did I know who was there? Did I care? Did I bleed? Hell, ninety-one people died, including the bride and groom.

Years later, after the establishment of Nefaria, he helped transform that site from one that recalled the slaughter of innocents to one that proclaimed the terrorists as heroes of the independence of Nefaria. He understood truth resides in perception not in reality.

That hotel bombing was my baptism. Then they blew up my son … oh, God, what horror was that … that defined my being. Day after day, night after night I thought of ways to punish them, 'Vengeance saith the Lord!' Hate drove every act. That made it easy when I became Prime Minister. Calculated, gradual erasure of Elusians … something they could sense, live through, suffer, despair about, that I designed, a corrosive and bitter humiliating defeat. I forced demolition of homes, thousands every year, forcing people into the streets weeping, a collective punishment that grew over time, and water, I seized their aquifers and gave it to my Pilgrims, virtually all of it, and left them, millions of them, with the remaining so they had to fight each other to get it. I watched their kids stand in line for hours waiting to fill a bucket while my Pilgrims played in their pools. I had laws drawn up to confiscate their land, huge segments of it, and I paid nothing for it. All I had to do was convince that idiot Emperor that Nefarians were victims of terrorists and he'd control the World Organization. I laughed inside; it's strange how much joy I got from manipulating their agony. And I'd think up new tortures like imprisoning thousands and never say why, and making it illegal for an Elusian to be married to a Nefarian. It became a game, how to lure everyone by telling them how I want peace when it's the last thing I want.

Now you stand over me, but I know you … know all three of you – Phala, Eshka, Harzia – cowards all. I strategize, I plan, I design the taking of the towns north of the old city. Not just shoot to kill … kill the minds … fear kills as well as bullets … drive them out, clean the towns of everyone. Surround them on three sides, drive them through the fourth; let them become the warning cry to the next town and the next. Kill those who will not leave. You don't gain land if people live on it unless they are your people. Force them out or bury them.

"When will they leave? Why do they keep posturing? Who are they impressing? He can't hear them. It's as though they want to taunt him. They're vicious men." Humilia suffers for her Patient while he, in the silence behind his closed eyelids, relives his accomplishments, his moments of retribution and glory.

****

Months ago, General Demas was rushed to the hospital from a banquet held to commemorate the beginning of a campaign that would propel him to a third unprecedented term as Prime Minister of Nefaria. His collapse threw the country into chaos. There was no one to replace him since he ruled as a dictator and had designed the country's policies for six years guiding it to unparalleled power in the region, a country both envied and hated.

Nefaria's future without the General remained uncertain. But as it became clear that he would not regain consciousness, the politicians grew bolder. Some decried his policies, others supported them. But the people knew that no one in the race had the charisma of the General or the connections that gave him his power.

That reality gave voice to countless editorials and commentaries about his six year reign and the regime he cobbled together to make it work. His alignment with religious fundamentalists and zealots alarmed the liberal sector, but they were powerless to prevent their ascent to the cabinet. As a result, ancient myths became political doctrine propelling the country into unending wars necessitating a military far greater than any of its neighbors.

Bastards. Standing over my grave, for God's sake ... as though I'm not here ... a sarcophagus carving in some ancient temple. I'm alive damn it! ... Oh, I want to curse these sycophants who grovel before power but have none. Incompetents chained by legalities and moral mealy mouthed twaddle. No wonder they fail. Listen to them ... they damn me. No, I don't follow orders.

What happens when I listen to politicians and poltroons? I slink away like some frightened chicken from what has to be done. I become them ... God forbid. Afraid that I won't forget, the manacle that stops action ... prevents victory. Remember only what advances victory ...

never need forgiveness. How's that for irony, you fools that slither to the worship hall begging for forgiveness? I create the sacred day that I knew ... no, that I know is a sham, a cruel joke. Do I know the necessity of slaughter in war? Do politicians? No. They need me, Nefaria needs me. Kindness has no place in war ... only the ruthless survive. Hate, one must hate.

As he curses his former friends from inside his dark prison, he knows in his gut that he attempted to conceal from his superiors what happened at the refugee camps years ago, but reporters got there before he could close down the area and published scathing reports of torture, rape and massacre. They described bodies crammed together like maggots swarming over rocks and piled garbage, troops standing outside the gates and on rooftops looking through binoculars as Nefarian mercenaries broke down the gates, scattered down the narrow alleys, two or three stopping at each entrance to the cement block homes, kicking down the doors, rushing inside, screams rising, intensifying, pulling bodies from the houses, stripping the women and girls, shoving them against the walls, fondling them, raping them, knifing them and leaving them strewn on the cobblestones, blood flowing from throats and bellies, the screams and shouts mingling into a cacophonic babble of helplessness and fear.

Days later the reports were even more detailed as a result of the public outcry that opened the refugee gates. Seasoned reporters quaked at the sight of naked girls, legs apart, eyes open in fear, frozen, a child's throat slit, the blood now caked around the tiny neck, rows of young men shot in the back; babies, now black from the sun's heat, swarming with flies, the rancid stench hovering above all, a hideous scene of piled bodies slowly decomposing in the intense heat that ricocheted off the white stucco, flies, flies everywhere; a baby girl shot from the back, her head blown away, lying next to her mother whose stomach was ripped open, slashed from side to side, her eyes starring in horror; and the boy, castrated, trousers torn open, flies swarming over his intestines.

But the Patient never repents or even admits responsibility for the massacres. He denies any wrongdoing blaming reporters for exaggeration and politicizing the killings at the refugee camps. Shortly after his outburst, he falls into a deep sleep.

****

"Thank, God, Carita, they're gone. They've been here for an hour, mumbling, yelling, but always condemning him. I thought he was their hero, their general. But they hate him. How'd he get so powerful if everybody hated him? I don't understand. The Ambassador, the one in the blue suit from the United Corporate States, he seemed surprised. He's apparently why they came. The generals know he's in a coma and not going to recover, but that man didn't seem to know that. Such a strange reaction."

"Well, I came in after they had talked for awhile. It seemed to me that the generals wanted to make sure the Ambassador knew that they were now in command and not the Patient. They'd just as soon have him buried."

"That one General said the Patient had demolished Elusian homes, bulldozed our fields, killed women and children. I hadn't heard that before. I knew the NOF did those things, but I didn't know he was responsible. Nanya says he's responsible, but I thought she meant he ran Nefaria, not that he did it. Maybe they just blame him for what they do."

"You told me once about your father. He was beaten by the NOF, right?"

"Yes, I was only 12 when it happened. We lived in Joyoa, north of here. This was before the Wall. But the townspeople knew it was coming so they demonstrated against it. No one could understand why anyone would build a prison wall around a village and cut the people off from their fields and friends. Even some Nefarians came out to join the townspeople."

"But if they were demonstrating peacefully and with Nefarians, how did your father get hurt?"

"Years after it happened he told me why. He helped organize the demonstration. I saw them come early to the house and drag him out before all the people showed up; they had others tied in a group behind the neighbor's fence. They beat them all, and I knew only later as a lesson not to oppose the NOF. They made it impossible for my father and the other men to organize demonstrations again. My mother went out after they left and carried him home with the neighbor, his knees bleeding, broken, his face in agony, sobbing with pain. I felt sick."

"Was our Patient there?"

"I don't know. They all wore black masks. I don't remember any faces. I was too young."

Oh, my angel, if you knew ... if you knew. Why do you let me know this now? I cringe at your story. I hear you weep. I feel your pain, my angel, my Humilia. I didn't know you then, years ago ... they were cockroaches from the swarm that crowded the dirt road that wanders through Joyoa. Any that oppose my orders suffer, any that defy me suffer for killing my boy. But now, I hear you weep for your father, a father I maimed.

I hear you cry inside. I don't want you to cry ... I confess I don't want to hear the sadness of your voice. I want the calm tones that you speak to me each time I hear you enter the room ... the sweet gentle voice that speaks to a dead man, a man you don't even know hears what you say. How I long to hear your voice ... without your sound I am not alive ... Silence surrounds my soul with the awfulness of an unbearable void. Oh, God, I lie here in a black universe, alive yet alone, the sole inhabitant of this emptiness without sound ... without comfort, without the touch of another human that I can feel ... isolated, alienated from every atom of existence except the fury of my memory that haunts the darkness like a specter of evil throbbing to life what I have done in life ... and cannot change ... cannot justify except to myself imprisoned in this carved skull that cries for release ... but there is no release, only the damned echo of my thought ricocheting through

my brain ... like shots from the rifles of an executioner's death squad.

Oh, my Humilia, I would it were not so. I wish I could hate you as I did when I first learned who you were. To have an Elusian care for me drove me mad. The word churned in my stomach like an acid. You were evil, you wanted me dead, any Nefarian; my boy, God damn it! Every black waking moment I spent despising you, and I knew nothing about you, nothing. But vengeance knows no reason. Impulsive hate reigns. So here I lie and think, think of you, wonder about you, why you do what you do. And irony of ironies, you know nothing of my thoughts. What if you ....

The Patient recalled events from the first year of his dictatorship, two years before he began construction on the infamous fence he designed to imprison the Elusians. But some Elusians understood what he intended and began a campaign to halt its construction. A number of towns and villages organized peaceful demonstrations to bring attention to the perceived consequences of the wall. The General moved at once to stop this protest before it spread and became news around the world. He went to Joyoa to make sure it became a symbol of his regime's ruthlessness that would not tolerate opposition to his wall. Nothing would stop his wall, not even the World Court or the World Organization both of which made formal condemnation. But The United Corporate States and its Emperor controlled the action that the WO could implement, and nothing happened to prevent the General from constructing his cement entombment wall around the Elusians.

Humilia left Joyoa when she was 17 to study nursing at the hospital. By that time the wall had been constructed. It slithered through the town cutting close to homes and animal shelters, slicing crop fields and olive orchards from the farmers' homes, making care and harvesting of their crops virtually impossible. Only one gate provided access to their fields, a gate opened only at the will of the NOF. Farmers could not take tractors and wagons through the fence, making the harvest only what a man could carry for two miles on his back. In the distance, but on Elusian land, stand the colonies erected for the Pilgrims. The wall allowed for expansion of the colonies since it enclosed 100s of dunams on the Nefarian side, making all the land fenced in confiscated land belonging to Nefaria.

The Corporate Ambassador, present at the morning gathering, the Honorable Janus Panderus, was a personal friend of long standing with Emperor Violentus of the United Corporate States. The two grew up together, went to the same university, joined the same secret society, played together at plush country clubs, and found total compatibility in their privileged lives. He, like the Emperor, had grown paunchy over the years, soft and self-indulgent. His appointment crowned a lifetime devoted to the Emperor, and, hence, he acts only to advance the Emperor's desires.

For six years he worked to keep Nefaria free from UCS interference and the main stream media indifferent to Nefarian policy against the Elusian people. The Patient worked equally hard to wrap the Ambassador in Nefarian State Awards, sumptuous banquets, and all the accoutrements that ensured loyalty to his policies. His reaction to General Phala's comment attested to his total absorption in the pleasures that attend the exalted position the Ambassador from UCS holds in Nefaria. For six years, he praised General Demas to the Emperor, to such an extent that the Emperor lauded him at a State dinner as a man of peace.

Ah, Humilia, I must have drifted off … I can't control how long or when I wake to consciousness. This life is not mine to control … I glide above the ocean floor on silent currents in a black sea … unseen … unable to see … an invisible spirit rising and falling in a soundless rhythm of unmarked time … a useless metronome swaying to and fro in eternal flow. How I yearn to yell, to explode beyond these paralyzed thoughts only I can hear, to pull back a curtain, confess to someone, anyone … if only to say, I'm here.

How deadly to obsequiously grovel before that nothing that grovels in turn before that clown, Violentus. Yet how necessary for my ends. Satisfy him and I pacify my Patron … keep him at bay … Oh, if he only knew or cared what I do. But such an idiot, surrounded by such cretins … I played him like a fiddle. Why should I worry?

I called to tell him I had to change plans … too many resistance attacks against Nefarians; need to delay the trip to Corporate City. Insidious, deceitful, call it what you will, but I needed to ensure the impact of the attack about to happen … yes, I knew the impending atrocity …

but I didn't tell him. Later I put my arm about his shoulder … told him we were victims in this war. We must pull our people under the same umbrella … I offered to help investigate, capture the criminals. Oh how he loved me. We became embattled brothers against unknown enemies. He adopted my methods … identify the resisters and those that aid them … charge them with crimes … attack and kill. I am the law and he must become the law; it's our duty, our right. It secures our people … and we have the means to inflict our will. He sang my praises and his obsequious Ambassador licked my boots.

What viciousness drives me? What's its source? What have I accomplished? Why do these thoughts gnaw at me now in this dark cave of my mind when I can see no light, no sun, not even a glint, a splinter of shadow … is the fullness of life what I have lived … driven by hate for any that oppose me … driven to force others to salute, to beg, to fawn before me … an ego lusting to taunt servility. Now that I lie here alone … what have I achieved, where is my ego now, where is my hate? What door does death open? What gate awaits?

The Patient slides back into his dark and desperate world as the evening shades envelope the windows making them mirrors reflecting the morbid scene inside his room. The final hours of the fourth day of the sacred season are coming to a close, yet he has no awareness of its passing save the presence of the Pilgrims who came on the third day. But he does not know the passing of days or hours, only hints that come from passing conversations, hints lost in the blackness of unconsciousness that when awake spring back to life or evaporate in the mist of lost time.

Yet not far away, the Pilgrims gather for the Confessional Procession to the Assembly Hall on Ypocrisis Street. Heavy clouds hang overhead and a light mist spreads like a blanket over the slow moving procession. Muffled drum heads absorb the measured beat that throbs slowly in time with the lamentation chant.

"I hear the voices of Judgment ring;

I hear the song the righteous sing."

"I see the sinners assemble before the throne,

Their faces filled with fear for a fate unknown."

"A pall of shame descends on this place,

For those without remorse are in disgrace."

The Pilgrims sway back and forth as they move in unison down the street, heads bobbing, closed fists beating their chests, their black coats moving rhythmically as though, in their suffering, they have become one body proclaiming their sins to their God. As the procession enters the decoratively carved doors of the Almighty's Hall, the swaying black forms appear to be sucked into the maw of a Medieval dragon that swallows its hapless victims, while the first faint wail of a ram's horn rises above the chant and swells into the night air blasting away the calm that accompanies the procession. That blast breaks the lifeless silence that engulfs the Patient, waking him to consciousness.

That sound, that screech growing to a wail, that lonely sound of the loon alone on some abandoned shore ... that signals the end of the fourth day, the Day of Confession. I know its purpose, I know my now ... what time it is, I created this time, this season of forgiving and retribution. What irony that it rings through these walls that enclose me, the very flesh that shrouds these thoughts.

What confession do I make? Do I take responsibility for what these Pilgrims do? Do their sins become mine, are mine theirs? What is sin if what they do happens because I bring them here and make possible what they would not have done had I not? Is the happenstance of politics the substance of sin? ... And who cares? Who judges? ... Thorthana's *Book o f Judgment* would not be held over them had I not made it the foundation of this sacred season. So is my God the God of Judgment? What nonsense that lets belief become truth when the source of that belief is fabricated ... No, I refuse to take on their guilt. I will not confess to allow them to hide from retribution ... Let them carry their own punishment; God knows they deserve it. I

don't believe, so what have I to fear even when I share their acts?

      The Patient slides once again into his nether world of dreams and visions sparked by memories of earlier days when he actively shared the NOF attacks against the Elusian villagers. He remembers the inquiry report that described the most publicized incident that he had to quell and his initial gut reaction to it which he put in his notes: "Stupid fool! Dead she's a martyr, wounded she's a deterrent."

      The report described in excruciating detail the action of the driver as he maneuvered his bulldozer forward, ever so slowly, an inch at a time, forward toward that girl with the bullhorn bellowing at him to stop demolishing homes. But he refused to stop. It appeared the driver would obey orders regardless of the consequences. He lifted the blade just above the dirt, moving slowly again, losing sight of her as the dozer rose up the mound then pushed through it, when she reappeared, her arms spread out in both directions with the bullhorn flying, and she disappeared again as the dozer rushed forward on the downward slope. He stopped, jammed the gears into reverse, and pulled back dragging her limp body beneath the blade till he lifted it and left her there in the dirt among her friends who rushed to her side screaming.

      Why do I think these things? ... I remember ... it's Confession Day, the end of confession day ... the Ram's horn made its blast. How funny to know the day ... well, not the exact day, a late fall day of sacred season. I don't

know the moon's cycle, but it has to be near the end of the year. Yet, this is the first time, actual time, I can connect with … that gives my existence a connection to others. Is that why I've rummaged through these memories? … Am I confessing? How strange a thought for me who never faulted my actions that are driven by a nature gifted to control. No guilt involved, mistakes happen but do not change nature … Besides, guilt's a human invention created to control, a handy device when garbed appropriately in the ritual of sacraments. I designed the sacred season for precisely that reason. So what does confession mean to the god who created both the sins and the guilt? … I should laugh at that, but what's laughter if none hears? What are tears if none sees? What is thought if none knows it exists?

How mysterious this turn of events … one day to speak and know the world listens, the next to think and the world pays no heed. I hang in this suspended death as deftly as the spider, between eternal nothingness and the awareness of it, only the spider can sense the wind disturb his being and I cannot. I seek in vain the exit from now and shudder at the thought that I will cease to be. Tomorrow … will I know tomorrow … will the Day of Penance come, will I know it when it comes … will recollection and suffering be my penance … followed by absolution, or will I receive no absolution and my fate forever will be unending suffering through recollection? What diabolical mind might conceive of such …

DAY FIVE

Penance

Ominous black clouds hang low over Desperia as the Day of Penance opens to oppressive beats of muffled drums summoning sinners to the assembly hall where all will publicly pray for forgiveness. Crowds of citizens line the streets to witness the display of suffering, most dressed in various shades of black, many with umbrellas opened against the drizzle that falls upon the scene. Pilgrims merge onto Ypocrisis Street from all the side streets, flow west toward the worship hall, striking a hand drum with a padded stick in time with the dull bass beat. The melancholy sound rises as the numbers increase and move slowly toward the west, a slow, meditative dirge that envelopes the city. Black banners with a golden circle totally a flame fall from the light poles up and down Ypocrisis Street as the faint wind keeps them moving in cadence with the mourners.

Humilia and Carita arrive at the edge of Ypocrisis Street just as the horde of Pilgrims pass. They are struck by the apparent sincerity of the penitents whose wet head scarves and long coats glisten in the glow of the early morning street lights as they bob and weave in unison toward the temple, a vibrant pulsating force resembling in the murky haze a slithering black snake. Humilia is visibly shaken by this scene. She turns to Carita who has noticed the sadness in her eyes.

"Last night, Nanya sat me down at the kitchen table. She said she had something to tell me that might explain why she had cried the day before. A tin rested on the table. She fumbled with its lid but then drew out newspaper clips. I couldn't tell what they were about until she started to explain. She was present when that Pilgrim, years ago, entered the Dijsam beside her home. She told me what happened. She had gone to the bathroom but returned to the hall that goes to the women's side. He had entered; he was ahead of her with a coat hanging over his left arm. What she saw has stayed with her to this day. He entered the prayer room, removed his shoes, moved quietly to his right and stood silently against the rear wall watching the bent over worshipers quietly murmuring their prayers, men and boys in clothes of many colors -- yellows, reds, blues, greens, browns – all on prayer carpets. Then she said he let the coat fall and lifted a machine gun and noise like she had never heard roared through the walls and dome as he spread his hate into the backs and heads of those unsuspecting worshipers. The silence burst into frenzied chaos of splattered blood, twisted bodies and screams of grief. She heard him call out the name of his God as the worshipers wrestled him to the floor. The papers, she pulled them out of the tin, reported that he died believing he had fulfilled the will of the Almighty. I could do nothing but hold her as she sobbed remembering that scene."

They turn toward the hospital hoping that their supervisor will forgive them for being late. They know they cannot accuse the soldiers of intentional humiliation and forced delay, although that is the truth, perhaps because they are sick of ten days of curfew and level their frustrations on the Elusians. But the soldiers enjoy making the young women take off their scarves and coats while the rain falls; they enjoy watching the girls pick up their paper bags that fall apart from being wet, with their lunches strewn on the muddy walk. And this day they made a young boy play his fiddle while the rain fell, laughing as the bow slid from the strings making a strident screeching sound.

When they arrive at the Patient's room, the drums sound soft and muffled yet quite audible. Humilia wonders if he can hear them, in fact, she asks the immobile form, "Can you hear the drums that call the Pilgrims to prayer? We watched them march toward the temple before we came this morning. We had no choice, the roads are closed off that we usually take."

"Humilia," Carita chimes in, "why do you talk to him? He can't hear you, it's silly."

"Oh, no, Carita, I believe he can hear. I can't know for sure, but I think God would not let him breathe for so many months without sensing His creation." And with that innocent outburst, she begins a quiet recitative of one of the psalms from her hymn book:

"I will praise all the peoples of the earth

With my whole heart;

I will tell all of your marvelous works.

I will be glad and rejoice in you,

And sing your worth before all the nations.

I will have no enemies among the nations;

None shall stumble or perish before me.

For I would not judge nor be judged

Nor have a God of judgment

Who would rebuke or destroy the peoples

Of the earth and blot out their lives

To exalt me above all others."

I hear you, my Angel, and the sweet tone of your song. How kind to sing even to the dead ... But who do you think you are to preach to me, for God's sake, you're just a servant girl? Such nonsense. How do I live with this? How do I push you out of my mind, how do I go back to where I used to be, how do I resurrect the hate I had for all of you, when you are the only person that gives me life, that let's me know someone knows I'm alive, that someone sings to a dead man. I wish I could see you, know your face as I know your voice, let you know how I feel. But it is not to be ... This God you call upon mocks me ... what else can it be ... I think, therefore I am not? Yes, I think, I think, I do

nothing else but think … and, now, my Angel, you cast this penance before me … have no enemies among the nations. But, my Humilia, all I have are enemies scattered throughout the world. I do the opposite of what your song asks … I hate Elusians, I despise the weak that beg me to stop the bulldozer from demolishing their home; I condemned and executed your Ammar who dared oppose me by hurling a missile into a crowded street killing him and the bystanders surrounding him; I send armies to destroy Nefaria's neighbors using flimsy excuses but claiming that we are the victims; I am the God you reject. I have created my world to exalt me, and … in the process … I have abandoned all that you find worthy.

But my innocent, you are only a victim of ancient teachings, as deceived as my Pilgrims who spend these seven days in recollection and suffering seeking in their faith reparation for guilt. For them, Humilia, it's an atonement I designed. No grand intelligence inspired me to write His words. It's my sacred season … designed to make Nefarians oblivious to guilt since none will feel the wrath of the Almighty's retribution if they but purge themselves in the water of absolution. Don't you see … God, you've lived it, your family's been devastated by it, your town's been deprived of water and fields … Don't you see they can inflict any cruelty, impose any punishment, enjoin any indignity, and know no retribution will follow. To be a Nefarian is to be guiltless as I am guiltless because we have lived so long as outcasts and victims beneath the boots of our oppressors. Don't you see, I use that fear of alienation, that gut wrenching pain in the victim's stomach to negate compassion for others.

I know the Nefarian mind, it's my mind after all, I know how to mold it ... to have fear, the instinctive fear of survival, propel acts that bury values and morals so deeply ingrained ... the only moral boundaries are those that secure the future of Nefaria. This idea I have made the driving force of Nefaria. Only we determine what is right; the world beyond ours cannot dictate to us any longer.

This is not your world, Humilia, this is the world bereft of caring, a barren wasteland where only the ruthless reside in splendor shut off from the weeping in the streets. The darkness in the world is not the mystery of the forests or the evil of the dragons, it is me, my mind ... my mind that gives meaning to the darkness even as I impose it on the innocent. We do not advance in wisdom, my Angel, we progress only in the brilliance and efficiency of our slaughter. Oh, sing, sing your psalms of kindness and forgiveness, but know the reason you wander over rocks and sand, a littered landscape of human detritus and waste, comes not from remission of sins, but from my pillaging of your water and land, my demolition of your homes, my theft of your businesses, my incessant harassment and humiliation of you ... don't you understand?

Why, Humilia, do I respond so to your voice? I don't even know who you are. Yet your sweet tone captivates me, the songs you sing to me lift my spirit. I've never thought before of you, of any of you, never wondered why you accept so little yet seem to have so much love.

Never before have I felt so close to someone, not even my wives, my children … Listen, she's singing again, no … both are singing so softly …

> "You shall join your brothers and sisters,
>
> In love shall you join them,
>
> For you will know that life is short,
>
> And Princes and all Powers, like People,
>
> Have but a moment in time
>
> To worship each other, while trembling
>
> Before the finality of existence."

"See, Carita, you can sense it when we sing, he does hear doesn't he?" Her voice is anxious yet enthusiastic as she looks intently at Carita with her deep brown eyes begging for confirmation.

"Oh, I don't know, Humilia. I hope it's so. How terrible to lie there day after day with no visitors, not even his wife. But if he hears, what does he think about? Does he talk only to himself?" Carita's questions seem to startle Humilia, but she says nothing.

Ah, sweet angels, your psalms are the chants of the powerless, of beggars, nomads that wander the byways of the earth, of those who live on dreams and hope, for they have nothing else. They sing the same refrains as Nefarians before they had a country, when they roamed through strange lands and bore witness to the suffering of others, when they condemned intolerance and injustice if only to ensure their own safety in foreign lands ... they, too, found oneness with all ... the helpless in the world must find comfort somewhere. But such naïve sentiments are not rooted in the beast. No ... no ... self interest drives our desires, not compassion. Compassion is a weakness ...and I loath weakness ... so why are you so intriguing to me? You know nothing about me; if you did you would hate me. But would you? Would you?

What line was that ... "To worship each other, while trembling/Before the finality of existence." How does a person worship another? I haven't had closeness with any person for fifty years that I'd want to worship. Such dribble. Always, always fighting with people ... tirades to my wife, scolding my kids, arguing and cursing officers and politicians ... constantly escaping from one or the other, lying to escape, to defend defiant actions against my superiors. Why worship any of them? What's to be gained?

Power is worshiped not people. No one worshiped me, even showed respect to me because I exuded kindness or concern ... no, they bent obsequiously because I could defeat them. Yet you come here every day, and talk to me. You have no fear; you don't just do your job, otherwise

why would you talk to me? How can someone so simple confuse me so much? ... Power makes caring and compassion for others obsolete. Caring and compassion, for God's sake, blunt power. Power is blind to compassion; it is its own reward and throws into the dustbin of discarded days the Samaritan and the saint. I can't hold a connection with those I oppress, I can't see them as equal to myself, I can't let Nefarians think such things ... Wait, they sing again ...

"My friends, we have learned from our past,

For to destroy only breeds destruction

Wrecking havoc on our children

And our children's children.

What once was can be no more!

'An eye for an eye, a tooth for a tooth,'

Is the road to extermination for those destroyed

And those who inflict the destruction."

"We should bring that psalm to the Pilgrims, Humilia. Maybe they'd really do penance if they paid attention to it." Carita half smiles as she nudges Humilia.

"Wait till tomorrow, Absolution Day. All will be out in force smiling and cavorting through the streets. Not one will be around for the Day of Retribution. I've seen this before. They don't think like we do, Carita, they don't blend with others or want to it seems. I don't understand it. They seem to believe they alone suffer and that is a wall between them and all others around them." Humilia's voice trails off in a quiet sadness.

There is something in your words, Humilia, that rings true. I shudder to go there though. I never thought I'd have the time or desire ... now I have time, desire I don't.

I've spent my entire life fighting the Elusians and any who supported them, but that required that I erase them from consciousness, exterminate them as people, turn them into terrorists ... a universal plague of vermin that crawl over *our* land infecting it with their destructive desire to eradicate us. I kill them as individuals and remake them as something that has to be destroyed. You were such vermin the day I knew you entered my secret life. Nothing you did or said to me erased that feeling of repulsion I had forced myself to live with, that I would never deny. But gradually, oh so gradually I let your voice wash over me, embrace me like a lover and I was no longer alone. Now my memories must live in the light of your eyes, eyes that see through your psalms, sung so sweetly to me.

And this psalm says both are destroyed, the vermin and the exterminator. The destroyer evolves into another being, a merciless, unconscious machine erasing not just the dijsams and homes and people of Elusia, but the innards of the Nefarian soul ... That I feel now ... a truth I would not admit before ... I create this reality. I tell our people

there are no innocents among the enemy, not old men, nor women, nor   children, none who can rise against Nefaria. Every person killed, every home destroyed, every school leveled, is a military target. Terrorism, I yell from the rooftops, must be rooted out.

I revel in this power. I twist our congenital fear of victim hood into a tyrannical virtue that turns oppression and hate into a justified reward ... given ... can one believe ... by our God to the chosen. Evil blossoms into good. Yet I know the barren wasteland I've created in our souls, a sterile place without mercy or contentment, only fear festering always, fear now not only of others but, more horribly, of self.

I know my tale is a lie, it's my trademark branded on every Nefarian's brow like the sign of the ancient angel that marked us as the chosen, the mark of fear seared into the skin, indelibly imprinted on our very souls ... Everything I do is wrapped in lies. I should be a "confessor" I know lies so well. I lie to the Emperor that we are brothers, victims of those who hate us; I lie to my generals to ensure they follow me adding just a touch of fear should they think otherwise; I lie to the press and force on them articles praising my actions written by my paid specialists in think-tanks I created. But there are lies I don't tell, lies of omission. I don't allow what I do to be seen; no outsider gets in to see behind my wall. Truth for the world is my truth ... perhaps what I have done to the Nefarian soul is like an infestation of cancerous cells that

spreads through out the body and rots it from within and they, like me, become the living dead.

How ironic that I arrive at this point, reflecting on penance and the world will never know, never suspect I thought such thoughts. I've destroyed the very people I set out to protect yet I'll remain always the fierce fighter, the relentless defender of Nefaria. Truth rarely sees the light.

Once again the Patient slides into his darkness oblivious for the moment of the bustling world that surrounds him. Humilia and Carita complete their chores, now in silence, reflecting on their own sense of alienation in the midst of these people who act perfunctorily toward them or ignore them all together.

"Come with me to the internet café, Carita," Humilia suggests, "I need to see if Ismaal emailed me before he left for Joyoa. I saw news on TV last night and the bombing of southern Elusia continues; it's gotten worse. I'm worried. They've been under siege for five months now."

"You mean the one at the other end of Despondah Street, the chocolate shop? I like that place. It smells so sweet and the computers are downstairs and private. Let's go."

Despondah Street is the main shop area for Elusians living within the old walled city. Heavy green doors border both sides of the alley, more an alley than a street, perhaps 12 feet across. Regardless, all the shops are pad-locked since the curfew is in effect for the duration of the sacred season. On Fridays the NOF sirens announce a three hour break in the curfew, time to allow the residents to get quickly to the shops for necessary items. At that time, troops flow into the streets to ensure that the shops are opened and the passage of people through the narrow lanes happens without incident. Ordinarily, the troops stay within the bunkers set at selected vantage points or on tops of the buildings up and down the alleys. Just before nightfall, soldiers in small groups, twos or threes, armed with M16s, move down the alleys to check that all is secure in the old city. No one is allowed in the streets who does not have an essential ID issued by the NOF. Both Humilia and Carita have such an ID because of their work at the hospital.

As they come within view of the shop, they realize it is not open, nor are any of the shops on either side. Humilia remembers that the last email she received from Ismaal was the day before the curfew. She hadn't thought of the curfew and the closed shops, so eager was she to hear from Ismaal. She would have to take the chance that he would make it to Joyoa. Without even looking at each other, they turn together and move toward Nanya's house.

DAY SIX

Absolution

Humilia rises early on this sixth day of the sacred season, anxious and agitated at the prospects ahead of her and the awareness that she must return by nightfall. She knows that she can return late and still get through the checkpoint because she has her ID that notes her work at the hospital, and most of the soldiers at the gate know that she cares for their general. The difficulty will be getting to the east side of the old city, to the side street where the small bus waits to take Elusians into the countryside. Should one of the soldiers stop her, they might find it strange that she is moving away from the gate to the hospital, not toward it. But she has an answer for that; she is going to meet a second cleaning girl, since Carita has this day off, to escort her to the hospital. That should work.

She dresses carefully in muted colors, a gray pleated jilbaab hangs about her ankles and a black ameera over her head and shoulders. Her shoulder bag hangs on her right side and holds the necessary water bottles, one for the ride to the village, the other for the return. The dust from the blowing wind always makes her throat itch, and even though the winter cold penetrates the air, the broken windows let the loose sand filter through. To get to the bus, she must stand in line under the corrugated tin, covering two chain link fences that serve as a narrow funnel to the NOF soldiers guarding the gate. Although there are only ten people in line when she arrives, all older women who work in the nearby city as cleaning ladies for Elusian Authority's offices, she must wait for more than a half hour. Two of the women are pulled from the line and told to strip behind a tin panel, placing their clothing in a pile on the ground. The soldiers prod the two with rubber truncheons to make them turn for a full inspection. It's become standard practice for the guards at the checkpoints to arbitrarily force women and men to strip. Humilia manages to avoid such humiliation since the line behind her has grown in numbers and the guards have to hurry before things get completely out of hand.

Once outside the wall, she hurries toward the bus which can be seen in the distance, smoke billowing out the back tail pipe sending black soot into the air. The street is narrow. Litter is everywhere: discarded ripped cardboard boxes, a broken wooden chair, dented water drums, bits and pieces of tar paper, old paint buckets, stacks of used wood panels, shreds of red and green cloth; a veritable garbage dump lines the street. It's almost six, and the stained brown bus is already full. She enters and takes the last seat at the back. There are twenty people, ten on each side, all are women, all dressed in long skirts and heavy coats, many with cloth bags on their laps, some are weeping. The floor of the bus is wet and muddy, some of the windows are cracked, two are broken at the top. If all goes well, she will get to Joyoa in an hour.

As the bus moves slowly beyond the wall and onto an unpaved road through an old neighborhood east of the city, the narrow byway seems to close in on the bus which has to navigate tight curves as it ascends the hill. Humilia nestles into her seat with her coat wrapped tightly about her neck. Outside the window, the monstrous cement wall rises 25 feet against the dark sky in the west. The bus crawls slowly down the crimped road weaving between parked cars, stalled donkey carts and the oncoming vehicles. To the right a glint of sunlight shows in the east as the bus moves parallel to the massive wall and north toward Joyoa. The dark clouds still hang above the city and the hills despite the early morning sun just topping the distant hills and the silhouetted block houses that stick like boxes atop the rise. On the edge of the road to the right, cubicle gray and white buildings line the street with shanty type appendages tacked to them as doorways or storage bins. Electric wires hang loosely overhead, some crossing over the wall where a tower of a dijsam rises in the distance, sliced off from the community it was built to serve.

The wall rises out of the road or appears to as it lumbers up the hill to the north. There is no curb, no sidewalk, no opening to the portion of east Elusia that exists on the other side. That portion of the east Elusian city is absorbed now into Nefaria providing expansion for the Pilgrims in the old city. As the bus moves north, the tower of the dijsam sinks behind the wall and the road begins to turn east, weaving first to the left then to the right making its way up the hill. The block houses appear attached as though stacked on top of each other at odd angles with some higher than their neighbor, each a varied shade of bleached white or acid gray. Many seem unfinished having steel rods poking above the cement forms that serve as the skeleton of the structure with cinder blocks stuffed between them. On the roofs water canisters sprout like stunted turrets laced with wires to hold them in place. Strewn everywhere are bits and pieces of paper, cans, garbage bags, corrugated tins and stacks of lumber, tarps, and clothes lines with a forgotten shirt blowing in the wind. This scene of egg crates with shadowed squares and rectangles marking doors, windows, and recessed areas formed by overhangs repeats itself on the right side as the bus driver shifts into second gear and turns again to the west. Jostled back and forth with the rhythm of the bus, Humilia begins to think about her Patient.

$$**********$$

At that very moment, he has stirred to life, inexplicably, since no sound has roused his consciousness. He senses that he's alone in the vast quietude that surrounds him. A primordial fear like that which haunts the lone hunter pursuing a wounded bear stabs at him, a fear he has not felt before in all the months he's lain immobile in his tomb of flesh. But now he wakes from a disturbing dream that clamps on his wakened mind like a vice.

He wakes in his dream to the "Dies Irae" lingering in solemn lamentation above the bowed heads of penitents in the ancient medieval church of the Almighty inside the old city of Desperia. The monophonic melody rises and falls in muted tones, a fitting dirge sung in requiem to the departed lying in the coffin at the foot of the altar, the tall orange candles standing at attention on either side, thick cylinders topped with flickering flames while the incense smoke drifts toward the groined vaults hidden in the darkness above the nave. His eyes open on this scene from the deep recesses of the dome where he observes all from the narrow walk way that circles its base. He looks into the coffin so far below and beholds his own face, eyes shut, hands carefully placed on his chest just below the cluster of ribbons that adorn his uniform. He recognizes no one in the pews, no familiar faces, no tears, no sorrow for the departed, only on closer view forms of cut out figures filling the seats, bent forms, heads lowered, faceless, lifeless images, mocking mirages of compassion and love.

Stunned by this scene that plays out below him, his mind moves down the darkened nave toward the west portal beneath the organ pipes that catch glints of light from candles and appear like dancing eyes glaring back. A lone figure enters from the recessed foyer, a figure framed by the shadows that fall in strips between the evening light filtered through the stained glass windows. The form moves forward silently, sheathed in a black cowl that falls to the floor, an image from the inquisition, frightening, fantastic in his imagined vision.

Yet something seems familiar about this figure, not because he has seen it before, but because he senses the presence, has known its thoughts, its unstated response to his very existence, its awareness of his being, its empathy for the horror of his predicament – the absolute blackness that envelopes him, the need, the terrifying need to break through, to see another, to lock eyes with another, to touch, to breach this wall of flesh, to be acknowledged. Then he knows, in one terrifying moment he knows it's Humilia.

She approaches the coffin, the candle flames sputtering their feeble light in the enormity of this vast vault that is his vantage place, circles around from the foot to the head that faces east and rests close to the altar steps. She pauses behind his head looking down at his bloated face, the bulging shut eyes, and the blotched skin. She reaches forward with her right hand to touch the eyes, a finger on each, and with her left hand covers his mouth as her head slowly looks upward toward the dome rimmed in suffused light as though she knows he stands there above viewing her below, and she quietly recites a psalm he had not yet heard her sing, her voice so muted he could barely hear, only the echo gently falling from the spandrels, "… no longer strangers." And in his dream his eyes opened and he could speak.

But the dream continues. He erupts from the coffin, dashes down the nave aisle out the western portal. The evening light haloes him in a golden hue of suffused light, a light at once soft, sumptuous, exquisite yet sacred as though God Himself had painted the scene. On he rushes toward the Almighty's Assembly Hall passing the white banners emblazoned with the three golden circles of the sacred season flying from the lamp posts and strung across Ypocrisis Street. He sees the Pilgrims ahead flowing into the Hall, garbed in white robes, carrying golden staffs adorned with the same banner, all singing the praises of the Almighty who has granted them absolution. None seem to anticipate the Day of Retribution.

But the Patient runs on, entering the Hall just as the last of the Pilgrims slides into the pews. As he comes into the light cast by the brilliantly lit interior of the Hall, the walls covered with white banners that hang from floor to ceiling etched with the three golden circles, he realizes that he, too, is now garbed in white, only he's in his hospital gown with the cerecloth tacked to his shoulders and billowing out behind him as he moves swiftly down the central aisle. He stumbles up the steps to the stage, turns to the assembled laity while waving his arms over his head to gain their attention. At first, few notice this stranger, then more and more until there is a sudden silence in the Hall of the Almighty.

He hears the silence, the pulsating, pounding silence that imprisons him day after day, month after month in his hospital bed, broken only by the clatter of a tray, the passing comment some voice utters, the lonesome echo of the ram's horn, and he presses his open hands against his ears as though some cannon's roar had split the hall and ricocheted against the granite walls. His bulging eyes stare back at thousands of eyes riveted on him, on their General, on the gowned patient in bare feet whose arms waved them to silence only to clasp his ears shut when the silence struck, an image of a raving lunatic demanding to be heard even as he opens his mouth to speak, but in the absurdity of this pathetic scene, no sound issues from his mouth as he carefully enunciates each word, revealing in his face the excruciating suffering he has undergone, and in his gestures the agonizing power of the confession that comes from his heart, a confession that is his penance through which he would have absolution granted him by the people he has destroyed.

I come to you through the power of an Angel who has broken the seal of silence that locked me in my black

tomb, alive yet dead, awake yet asleep, conscious yet unconscious, forgotten, isolated, alienated from family, friends, countrymen, the sad and pathetic figure of your indifference, your sin of omission, the most devastating of all the sins against humanity, to erase existence from memory.

But I do not come in anger, I do not come to berate you, I do not intend to mock you or insult you, I come to you contrite of soul seeking from you remission of my sins, for I am the cause of your sinfulness, of your inhumanity, of the very indifference I encouraged in you, the immorality I taught in all the acts I committed, gross, vile, insidious, heinous acts against our brothers and sisters, twisting the reality of their barbarity into virtues to be extolled, and in the process infecting you with my evil that has spread like a cancer throughout the body of the Nefarian state, rotting it from the inside so that you did not see how empty and black were your sins and your corruption.

I fall before you seeking your forgiveness for I have sinned. Oh, my brothers and sisters, I have slain the child clasped in its mother's arms, I have hurled missiles into crowded streets and exulted at the carnage leashed upon the innocents, I have forgotten friends and family, my very own children to gain power over all, I have buried the teachings of our prophets beneath my feet as I abandoned all for my glory. I weep now that you may witness the agony of my suffering. Forgive me, forgive me.

As the Patient stands in the glare of the lights now turned upon the stage, the ridiculous appearance of this figure in his hospital gown that hangs loosely from his neck to his knees, with the cerecloth swaying back and forth as he marches slowly from one side of the stage to the other, with his arms raised in supplication, his eyes intensely looking at the congregation with a penetrating glare that literally condemns them for acts they do not comprehend, all in the assembly hall rise in anger at this fat stumpy man, this madman that roams about the stage with arms flailing, and they rush the platform grabbing at him as they attempt to usher him through the curtains at the back of the stage.

All the time he stands before them, all the time he marches up and down the stage, he harangues the crowd with his fists, beseeching them to hear, waving his arms, screaming at the top of his lungs so the whole assembly can hear – yet no sound issues from his mouth. Not a word is heard, not a person reaches out to touch him in kindness, no person looks at him with compassion; he's alone again, and his aloneness finds refuge in the silence of his immobile body clothed in his white gown covered by the cerecloth, his eyes closed, his mouth taut and shut, his fingers flat and motionless on his chest, the almost inaudible click of the heart monitor the only sound, his form that had observed this entire episode from the rim of the dome, back home in his walled tomb.

An abrupt turn in the road jostles the bus and wakes Humilia from a brief but uneasy sleep that had begun with thoughts of her Patient alone without her for the first time in months, but now turn inward as she feels an unexplainable urgency forcing her to move through shadows toward a burial vault visible at the end of a long hall way, a place she does not recognize and cannot explain. She experiences a sense that her Patient has contacted her though she does not know how or why. But the scene outside the bus interrupts these thoughts as she recognizes the refugee camp that is only fifteen minutes from Joyoa.

The camp spreads out along the roadway to the right of the bus, its narrow alleys barely wide enough for a car to pass as they slide awkwardly into the unpaved road her bus travels. Box-like buildings stand at the corners making it impossible for a car to enter without pushing into the oncoming traffic. Graffiti scars the walls of the brownish cement that is plastered with ripped posters and old banners that now whip in the wind as the bus passes by. Electric wires hang from poles across the alleys to neighboring buildings while clusters of other wires run zigzag from pole to pole up the hill. Water tanks dot the roof tops that overlook the debris below. Discarded couches, junked cars, garbage buckets and rubble are pushed against the walls, a constant reminder that the Nefarian occupiers impose taxes only to withhold them from Elusian authorities.

Kids run in the alleys. Others stand against the walls, their yellow and pink shirts and blouses blending into the blotched remnants of weathered paint and the remains of posters. Humilia notices the streams of water that flow down the alleys into the road and form muddy ruts through which the children run. She recalls the day she left Joyoa for Desperia years ago and thinks how time has frozen this place; nothing changes, the ugliness appears constant like the black clouds that have hovered over Desperia since the Day of Awareness began the seven days of the sacred season. It's all so depressing, dreariness without end, so complete it seeps into the soul like the draining water that slides down the alleys into the ruts below.

Now fully awake, only minutes from her home, her excitement increases in anticipation of seeing Ismaal for the first time in years, and her mother and, with trepidation, her father who has withdrawn so completely as though he silently blames everyone, the townspeople, the other beaten men, his own family for his crippled state. She reflects on how transformed he's become since the occupation came so visibly to Joyoa with the building of the wall. Nothing is as it had been. No one can enter or leave without permission of the NOF; no one can cross through the fence to get to their olive trees or crops without waiting for the gate to open at exactly the time set by the soldiers; no one can even wear a shirt if it has markings that a soldier objects to, an 18 year old boy or girl can order a father or mother around, even an old man who has lived four times as long. Nothing is as it should be, she muses, as anger swells with the thought.

The bus reaches a rise in the road as it enters the little town of Joyoa which slides casually down the slope toward the west where the sea can be seen in the distance. Humilia sits up now attentive to the familiar buildings on each side and the slow pace of her neighbors who move in and out of the shops stopping to wave or talk with a friend. She smiles unexpectedly as she feels the warmth of her home embrace her. A knock on the window intrudes on her thoughts; she turns to see Ismaal running beside the bus, his dark beard a surprise to her, his whole demeanor that of an older man, yet with the enthusiasm of youth as he yells above the bus engine for Humilia to get out. The driver has caught sight of him in the mirror and brings the bus to a stop. She rushes to the door and jumps into his arms, crying now as the flood of tears erupts to fill the missing five years. The driver waits a moment, then throws Humilia's bag to Ismaal before continuing on his journey.

The two amble slowly down the street waving to a neighbor sitting outside the small deli, nodding to the butcher who comes out to greet them, turning again and again to each other drinking in the smile, the happiness in the eyes, the joy of this brief reunion. Ismaal leads Humilia to the bakery shop on the corner, a small place with its half door open, the glass case filled with croissants still hot from the oven. They sit outside on the low wall next to the street drinking tea while they eat and talk.

"What did you think when you first returned," Humilia asks, her tone betraying the expected answer. "How different was everything?"

"You know what's changed and you certainly know what I feel. These last few moments, just that slow walk down the street with you, the quiet laughing, holding hands, just seeing you again, the way it used to be years ago, that's all gone now. You know that, I know that. We live in a cage; there's no free movement. We just had all we'll get today, just those moments. The moment we open our eyes we see the wall surrounding us like some steel belt. How do I feel? I hate it." Ismaal stares out to the west, toward the distant sea to what used to be when he was young the promise of dreams, where all that he longed to do could be fulfilled. But now, both his eyes and his tone convey the isolation, the powerlessness, the despair that encircles him as completely as the Wall.

"Last night, just after I got back," he continued. "Cynd, you remember him? He's about 12 now. He saw me and shouted my name. We started talking. You know what he said; it fits what I've just been saying. His folks got a letter from the NOF. They ordered his father to tear down the sheds he's had forever to cover the goats, chickens, and the donkey and cow, those old sheds of broken palettes and tin. You know what I'm talking about? You know why? Because they are too close to their fence, that monstrous steel pen they've surrounded us with using his land that they never paid for. Now the shed that's been there for years is too close. No offer to pay for a new shed much less pay for the land they confiscated. Just tear it down or they will. How do you live with that?" The anger was palpable as he recounted Cynd's story, told by a boy he had known all his life, a kind gentle kid that could not understand why the NOF acted that way.

"I remember Cynd and his mother. They've got some of the oldest olive trees in Joyoa on that land, or they did. I don't know how many were bulldozed down, but I know one that's a thousand years old sits just outside the shed closest to the wall. That was terrible when they cut down all those trees to build that monstrosity. I know what you are saying, but we've got to have some good moments together, Ismaal, please," Humilia pleads.

"Ok, let's go home so the rest of the family gets some time with you."

"Yes, but I want to know what you are doing down there. What jobs have you had, how do you survive? Have you had encounters with the Pilgrims and the NOF?"

"I've got stories you won't believe, stories that will make you cry I'm afraid. There's no other way to tell it. I've lived it, but I don't understand it."

The two make their way to the right, going east toward their home that sits in a cluster of single story boxes nestled around the elementary school on the edge of town, most have a small gravel yard enclosed with a stucco wall about three feet high, some with sheds for a goat or donkey, a few with a dusty, dented car or small pick up outside the opening in the wall. As they walk, Humilia notices that Ismaal walks with a slight limp, and for the first time looks at his clothes that are worn and dirty. She sees that he's strong; his broad shoulders push against his black coat pulling it taut so that it reflects the shine that comes with wear on the elbows and cuffs. The dark blue winter skull cap pushes his black curly hair out so that it falls around the collar making him appear larger than he really is. Beneath the beard, the face appears thinner than she remembered, the lines from the nose visible now, and the cheeks sunken. But it's his eyes that strike her. They're deep set yet bright because the rich brown pupil is rimmed with black and set against the glistening white of the eyes. She feels the intensity of his look, the attentiveness, watchfulness, the total awareness to all about him, as though he never rests, as alert as a cat caught in a strange yard.

"You're walking home with me, but you're in some other place. What are you thinking, Humilia. You've been silent."

"I'm sorry, Ismaal, but I just thought how different our lives are. I'm looking at you for the first time in years and realize what different paths we've taken. Your clothes, the limp, and your eyes, the depth of your eyes tells me you've seen things I can't imagine. I've lived a sheltered existence. I just have to keep to my routine, avoid them as much as I can. Get back to Nanya and my friends. But you ... you're someplace else, somewhere I fear to go. Forgive my silence, Ismaal, please," Humilia speaks quietly as she confronts for the first time this division between them, thoughts that open doors she had not known would open this day.

Within the hour, Humilia understands that her return to meet with Ismaal had become a neighborhood event. Neighbors sit in every chair, on the sofa, and around the table next to her mother and father. She stands in the doorway between the living room and the kitchen watching Ismaal as he responds to questions. He's seated across the room against the wall where he can see her, aware that he came to see her, aware that she is now old enough to grasp all he will say. The small house becomes Joyoa's assembly hall where citizens listen to a voice from faraway places, a voice like that of ancient prophets telling stories of suffering kinship lest they forget and sink into the indifference that marks the brow of their oppressors. But Ismaal looks nothing like an ancient prophet; his gestures, the vibrancy of his voice, his alertness give life to his zeal and youthfulness.

While some drink tea and others hold small water bottles, Ismaal describes where he's been in the south and how he survived the first few months until he met, through the help of friends, those working in the human rights offices preparing eye witness and statistical reports on injuries and deaths, house demolitions, checkpoints, land confiscations, imprisonments and torture for international rights organizations who were not allowed to enter the southern regions of Elusia. Because of these activities, the NOF spends great amounts of time trying to find the Elusians who work for EHRA, sending them off to jail whenever they can in the vain hope that they can suppress the reports. As he spoke, Humilia noticed that her father sat up in his wheel chair, attentive to what Ismaal said and seemingly proud of his son that had left five years before, within a week of his own humiliation and beating by the NOF. Perhaps, thought Humilia, he sees himself in Ismaal.

"I brought many reports with me," Ismaal noted as he continued his narrative of his adventures in the south, "but I wasn't involved with all of them. Each of us goes out every day to be a witness somewhere; many times we have information brought to us of something that will cause problems and make the NOF react. Like peace sit-ins or demonstrations against the wall somewhere. We go there so we can gather information and watch what takes place. Sometimes we can get things on camera or even video, but many times the NOF grabs the camera so it gets expensive. But other times it's accidental, things that happen we didn't know would happen. And all the time, you have to act innocent. I can't even intervene in most cases because that would end my effectiveness. The reports are the only way to let the world know what's taking place. But even that's being undermined as the Nefarians publish their own documents that omit information but throw into question the validity of our reports."

"Why's that allowed? Why can they control everything like that? Don't the WO and the people in the Corporate States know better? Can't they see what's happened?" The speaker's indignant tone caught the attention of the people in the room who responded with "yes … yes" and "true, you're right." Ismaal sympathizes with their reaction and tries to explain what, in fact, they already knew: the outside world lives in ignorance because the elite who control, the government of

Nefaria and its Prime Minister, General Demas, determine what will be published and what will be hidden. They control not only in Nefaria, but in the UCS through their lobbies who ensure that congressional representatives fear loss of their position if they attempt to thwart the will of the Nefarians.

"Let me give you an example," Ismaal continued, "an example I actually saw take place although I was just outside the door with a lot of others, neighbors of the family that was being harassed by the NOF. More than harassed as it turned out. Let me explain. The NOF wanted a suspected terrorist in this crowded tenement, right in the middle of the refugee camp. But they had the wrong house. They didn't know that and didn't care, quite frankly. They broke through the door – that's how I heard about it because I had just turned the corner and saw them do it – grabbed an older man, he turned out to be the father of 11 children in that home, shoved him against the wall outside, yelling at him, right in his face. And all the kids are standing there crying watching their father getting beaten.

We've been there haven't we. It made me think of my father, Avram, who sits right there and knows what I'm saying. Anyway, the yelling and beating got worse; he never said a thing, so they beat him more. The kids were screaming, 'He's deaf, he's deaf,' but they didn't understand. After a while, the mother pushes through the soldiers, waving her hands and placing them over her ears trying to show them what they didn't know. And she yelled, 'He's deaf, he's deaf.' By this time they were irate, totally out of control.

The leader took out his pistol and shot the mother! Shot her. Not once but three times. She fell to the floor. No one expected that. We all yelled for an ambulance. Take her to the hospital. The kids were going insane. Their mother lying on the floor, moving slightly, blood pouring from the side of her head. They pushed us out of the way. They refused to call an ambulance but someone on the edge of the crowd ran to call one. An hour later they let her be taken. She was already dead. You know how that was reported? 'NOF forces met resistance in southern Elusia yesterday, a few terrorists were killed including a civilian woman killed by a tank round.' You know where that appeared? In only one sentence in 3 papers in the UCS, in a small column on a back page. Nowhere else. Can you imagine how that would have been reported through out the world if Elusians had done that to Nefarians! Does that answer your question?"

"It certainly does, but it doesn't tell me what you can do about it. What happens to those kids? Who takes care of that family now? Who talks to the father? Who feeds that family? How do the kids live with what they saw? Shall I go on?"

"No need to my friend. It's worse than you think. How's this. The Nefarian's have convinced the WO by controlling the delegates to that body from the UCS that local human rights groups sympathize with terrorists by giving aid to them and their families, so now no money can come through that organization to us. It makes no difference to them that helping this family helps no terrorists because they need to claim for their reports that the father was a terrorist suspect or collaborator. None of their money can go to help them. That's the same thing with helping those whose house has been demolished because a son or cousin living with them committed a terrorist act. Collective punishment may be outlawed by the international community, but it isn't in Nefaria. In fact, it's routine."

As the conversation proceeds, Ismaal becomes more and more intense. His forehead beads with sweat, furrows form above his eyes, and his voice rises. Humilia realizes this gradual change. She worries but knows also that he's bringing to these people an awareness of what they will face as the days and months go by. The strangulation taking place in southern Elusia will happen in Joyoa in due time and Ismaal's emphasis on the indifference of the people that could change the conditions he reports prepares them to abandon dreams of altruism and human sympathy. In his mind, and in her growing awareness, it's a Nefarian world that rules and rules ruthlessly. Knowing that prepares the mind, if not the heart, for the suffering yet to come.

"Let me return to how they control what gets to the outside world. Our office was raided two weeks ago by the NOF. They wanted some of us, but we knew they were coming and left. But here's what they did to a peaceful organization; and again this is breaking international law. But, then, in Nefaria there's no law but their law."

"Remember to mention how this was reported," said the original questioner.

"It wasn't! This is so common in the south that it's never reported. But this is what happened. The NOF showed up, occupied the offices for a few hours, smashed, burned and broke every computer we had, heaped the terminals on the floor and threw some into the yard from the back window, cut the electric cords, removed the hard disks, stole the supplies – disks, lap tops, phones – and burned our reams of paper. Then they shit on the tables and desks, pissed on the doors like dogs leaving their marks on trees and fire hydrants. And they wrapped all this up with graffiti filled with gross words that called us cockroaches and vermin sprinkled with words of hate. That's the behavior of a religious state filled with worshipping Pilgrims that even now are celebrating their sacred season of, thank God, forgiveness and retribution. I always wondered why they didn't celebrate that season in Elusia." Ismaal's sarcasm turns caustic, but even so it is appreciated by those present.

"I need to know how you feel about these kids in their uniforms that make up the NOF. They're just teenagers yet they act this way. How do you explain that? No one at your office was there. They didn't get angry at you. Where'd the hatred come from? Who told them to behave this way? Would the citizens of UCS let their kids do these things? Do they teach their children to hate us also? They don't even know us."

This lament came from an elderly woman sitting beside Humila's father, a neighbor who lived two doors down and had been at the beating of her father years ago. She tried to remember her name, and then it came to her, Sagacita. She recalled that she had tried to intervene against the hooded figures who lashed at the group of men that had organized the demonstration. She asked them why they acted like animals, what drove them, fathers of families to destroy another family's father. But they ignored her, just shoved her aside. They were beyond reason; brute force is all they knew.

"Oh, Sagicita, I wish I knew the answer to that. I see what they do, I hear what they say, I even smell what's inside them, but I don't know what drives them. That's something they must answer for, and I don't mean to their God. From what I've read, their God tells them to do these things. What kind of a God is that? So that's no explanation for me. But you put your question in an intriguing way: 'Do they teach their children to hate us?' I hadn't put it to myself that way. But if they do, what could they possibly tell them that would make them hate people they never met. I mean we tell kids to avoid strangers when they ask you to do something like ride with them, but we don't tell them to hate them or kill them."

"I don't mean to interrupt, Ismaal, but there's more to it than that, isn't there?" The old man speaking sat in the corner of the room. Humilia was watching him at times as he sat with his head bowed, eyes closed, yet awake. She knew he listened so was not surprised when he spoke.

"You dismissed the religious teachings, yet if the Nefarians are taught to destroy others because their God has chosen them above all others, and if he commands through the Divines that we are enemies, then wouldn't the parents have to teach their kids to kill? Under those conditions, whatever the religion, who is to blame? How can we, how can the people of any country convince otherwise those who are taught that they alone are chosen from believing what their ministers tell them God tells them? That's a confusing way of saying it perhaps, but it shows us the problem is beyond solution."

"Ah, Cautio, I should have expected you to raise that issue. You're far smarter than I am so you'll have to answer that yourself. I live in the practical world, the day to day atrocities that fill our lives. We live. If God made the world, he also made us to live in it. I don't buy chosenness. Certainly it contains the contradiction of God in its very supposition. He becomes both Savior and Satan, an oxymoron, I'd suggest. You either believe in a God that is a God or you don't. But don't create a contradiction and bless him as true. So says Ismaal, Cautio! Is that an answer?"

"A better one than you might have patronized me with when you were here last, my Son. Time wears well on you. Let me bless you before you return."

"I would be honored. Indeed, your blessing might protect me against the on-going rain of bombs and missiles that the NOF hurls at us, especially Elusia City that they appear to especially hate. Day after day they send F-16s to fling their screaming missiles into our buildings. Day after day the sonic booms of those planes crash through our heads, the heads of kids, children who run and hide with their hands over their ears. Frightened out of their minds. Done intentionally, over and over. And why? Because our terrorists send feeble rockets into their territory that hit nothing, a gesture to tell them they occupy our land illegally, what any people would do to spit at their oppressors. Spit and stones … that's our military hardware. They act like we're the Russian army fighting a weak force trying to protect itself against a ruthless and determined enemy. Such nonsense."

At this point, Ismaal rises and excuses himself as he goes to the bathroom. Humilia moves to provide additional tea and croissants. There's a general rustling among the guests until he returns. It's as though his stories have renewed for them their connection with their families in southern Elusia for it's the reality of families of Elusians that binds them together in the suffering that has been their lot for almost sixty years.

"Ok, my friends, let's continue. I needed that break. Thanks. There's so many stories to tell, I don't know where to begin. Now you can get a lot more information from these reports and they explain a lot that I haven't covered, especially the calculated killing of medical personnel, ambulance drivers and nurses. Why would they target such people? That's even worse than random killing because it prevents healing of those they've already shot. It doesn't make any sense, yet somehow they explain it to themselves. But let me tell you one of the weirdest things I've been directly involved with."

"Three months ago this happened. I was aiding the driver of an ambulance called to a neighborhood to evacuate a woman and her three children who were injured and inside their house. A number of NOF were in the area when we arrived so we stopped about 50 metres from the house. The driver pressed the horn to notify the people in the house to bring out the injured. We couldn't get closer because of the NOF. The driver tried to talk on the cell phone to the Ministry of Health to explain the situation. We were told to wait until the military would let us get closer. Instead, in about five minutes, the tanks fired on us. They didn't hit us but we had to retreat. A few minutes later I saw a bulldozer and a tank coming towards us, one in front the other behind where we stopped. The bulldozer operator began to push sand and gravel in front of the ambulance while another came behind and shoved demolished debris from houses behind the ambulance. We were caught behind hills of sand and debris. One of the bulldozers hit electric wires that fell on the ambulance. Now we were trapped inside. But we tried to open the doors, and when we did the tanks fired at us. They sat there laughing at our predicament, but there was nothing funny about it. We were terrified. After three hours we were told we could leave. The bulldozers removed the barriers. We had to leave the area without the injured. That's an example of NOF health care for the people under occupation. How do you explain that?" By now, Ismaal's voice had grown quieter yet more somber and sardonic. The anger and frustration he kept hidden slowly came forth as his tales of human horror continued, a trail of imposed arrogance and humiliation on those victims who had to endure the suffering.

"You know, Ismaal, it's the consistency of the behavior that's astonishing," Sagicita commented, "a consistency of meanness that denies that a person is suffering or being hurt by what they do. Some actions are trivial like insults thrown at kids going to school, but others are more insidious, diabolical like the one you just recounted. They laughed while that mother and her kids suffered and you and the driver placed in jeopardy. That's a meanness that denies people are people; no regard for another, none whatsoever. Where does that reside? What minds are capable of that behavior? They are in no danger, so it's not fear for self. It's not personal animosity against someone that has attacked them; they don't know the people they treat so cruelly. I know of no animal that torments other animals for sport, unless it's a cat playing with a mouse. Are we to compare ourselves to that?"

"Sagicita, how people can treat others that way I do not understand. I can explain why some of our people attack them, even those who kill themselves to destroy some of them. At some point, when you've witnessed your father beaten without mercy, seen your neighbor's house bulldozed down, seen land stolen and trees uprooted, watched tanks, F-16s, humvees, and thousands of heavily armed soldiers swarm over a refugee camp killing anyone in sight, heard from a friend about torture, a hopelessness sets in, a desperation that buries logic, compassion, any principles that one has lived by for years, and in absolute frustration the indifference about who you kill overcomes all else, and the innocent suffer at our hands. Yet, terrible as that is, I understand it. I can't understand what they do; it's beyond my understanding. Perhaps they carry suffering deep inside that I cannot see; they seem to have everything, yet they lash out at those they don't know for some reason. Some hopelessness they know and feel? I don't know.

"Let me cite one more horrific example. It's striking in its clarity of intent and total dismissal of the people affected. I did not witness this; it came to us from a journalist who wrote of it in great detail. A 17 year old girl was preparing for her final exams. She studied in her bed room upstairs, walking back and forth as she memorized material. The room was brightly lit. You have the picture? A young girl pacing back and forth in full view through the window to anyone outside. Well, outside on an adjacent rooftop sat a NOF sniper. That sniper pinpointed his target with such accuracy that he killed her with one bullet in the center of her forehead. That's blatant murder. Needless to say, he was never charged. I tell you that without the turmoil within that home, the mother rushing to the door, the blood dripping over her book, the family torn apart, because I want to focus on the act. Deliberate, calculated, the achievement of a trained skill taught by one man to a teenage soldier who did what he was trained to do. No thought about the girl, her work on the exam that could open her life to fulfill dreams, no thought about the mother or father and how they would live the rest of their lives without their daughter knowing she was target practice for some kid trained by the occupiers, no thought for the neighborhood, the kids that went to school with her, the families that now had added fear for the next day and the next since meaningless, random brutality is as possible as tripping over a curb stone. I'm not sure 'meanness' is the word. There's an arrogance that exists in the innards of these people that corrodes any feeling of community or commonness of existence between them and everyone else that walks the earth, especially Elusians."

Ismaal's voice quavered at the end of his story as though this clarity of act revealed for him the futility of his life now that found some purpose in witnessing, recording, and cataloguing the inhumanity of the occupation. If the world outside knew nothing of their plight or worse still if they knew of it but didn't care, then what purpose did his work serve? If the world knows only what the oppressors reveal, then the reality of the Elusian people does not exist. They are what their oppressors say they are, a people who exist in the fiction created for them though it bears no resemblance to their day to day lives.

Those listening to Ismaal felt his frustration. All remained silent waiting for him to return to his narrative. But Humilia suddenly realized that she could not stay any longer. The bus back to Desperia left in half an hour. Desperately, she signaled to Ismaal by pointing to her wrist. He understood. He called for a brief break so he could say good-by to his sister. The neighbors left the room so that the family could spend some moments together. Ismaal went down on his knees beside his father as Humilia and her mother stood behind him. Avram put his hand on Ismaal's head, a gesture that recognized his coming of age and his elevated position in the family. The son had taken on the burden of the father. Humilia hummed one of her psalms, "They filled my spirit to overflowing; I wanted for nothing./They restored my soul with the honor they bestowed on me." as the family drew together in a final embrace.

Ismaal walked Humilia to the gate remarking to her as they walked that she was caring for the Prime Minister of Nefaria, a calling beyond what most condemned to their insidious and diabolical existence would be able to do. She did what every human should do, care for another, even the enemy.

"Humilia, I left Joyoa a young, bitter man determined to wreak death and destruction on the Nefarians. I'd kill Pilgrims in the south to punish those who beat our father. I had only vengeance and hatred in my heart. But I met and worked with those who recruited young boys to become martyrs of Elusia, and I witnessed the void left in those young kids – whatever might have been closed down forever, dead before they could live. It didn't take long to know that vengeance cures nothing; it's only a breeding ground for more meaningless death. That's why I turned to witnessing for the human rights groups. It doesn't rid me of hopelessness, but it offers the only way to open eyes beyond Elusia so that some will know the truth. Perhaps in time hope will return. You have chosen a work that goes beyond what I do; you feel for one you have every reason to hate. But you sense what he should have so many years ago; he's not alone in the world if he but opens his heart to another. You've given him a chance to know that, if he lives at all, and no other gave him that chance when he walked the streets of Nefaria. Stay safe; stay as you are."

They embraced just before Humilia ran to the bus to return to her Patient.

DAY SEVEN

Retribution

Low menacing clouds move over Desperia from the west as the Day of Retribution opens with the rumbling peal of deep throated bells, a threatening tenebrous tone that mirrors the gloom of the darkened sky. The streets are empty except for the black banners studded with ringlets of flame that rise high above the poles in the winter's wind. For seven long days the melancholy weather hovered over the city casting a funereal pall over the rituals of the sacred season. Even the Day of Absolution was bathed in a light mist that washed over the celebrating Pilgrims as they danced in the streets in their white robes chanting ancient songs of acquiescence and honor to the Almighty judge who had absolved them of guilt. Now on this final day when the Almighty God of Thorthana wields his ultimate judgment before His people, when the felt presence of Retribution's power hovers in the canopy of the night sky like some impending doom, the Pilgrims have fled the city lest they be seen as sinners that must face the wrath of the everlasting God.

Up and down Ypocrisis Street the banners whip in the frosty wind emitting piercing sounds as they snap, creating a rhythmic beat against the endless tolling of the bells. All else is silence; no somber chants, no thumping of the breast, no weeping disturbs the seventh day. The street lies empty, the glass windows on the tall buildings, two stories high, reflect the gray morbid atmosphere that envelops the street while the repetitive pealing of the bells echoes down the cavernous canyon toward the Assembly Hall of the Almighty. The enormous doors open to the empty hall where the white banners that had adorned the walls no longer hang, instead huge black banners fall from the tops of windows inscribed with the ever present flaming circles of retribution. Thousands of candles flicker from semi-circular lamps that line the aisles adjacent to the windows and, on the stage, enormous thick candles for the dead stand in solemn tribute to the Almighty who must render the judgment of retribution on those who without remorse slaughter their kin, on the treacherous who use their gift of reason to thwart the desires of their Creator, and on the fraudulent, on hypocrites, on deceivers, and on sowers of discord who for personal gain deceive friends, family and country.

But the empty hall tells all, a hollow mockery of the season they extol. The Pilgrims admit of no fault, no guilt that casts them against their God. Theirs is an occult isolation that surrounds them with innocence since they are of the chosen, an ancient belief that fosters an inclusiveness of privilege built on tradition and ritual, a virtual language of personality, distinctiveness, the mark of uniqueness impressed from the beginning of time. None can enter this special realm that specter like circles those so blessed and, by implication, barricades all others from their sanctuary of Almighty favor. Only those born to the right receive approbation, admittance to the hall of favor, the exclusive benediction that banishes guilt by very virtue of birth, casting all not of the elect into inferior states of human degradation. Such privilege breeds insensitivity, callousness and indifference that, in turn, is a wall barricading the Pilgrim from engagement with his fellows and an impenetrable barrier that gives birth to resentment, fear, and revenge. A hundred and seventy years ago, a moralist from another time caught the severity of this consciousness in hearing the words of another bound in blood to these Pilgrims: "I fancied ... that there was a bitterness indefinably mingled with his tone, as of one cut off from natural sympathies, and blasted with a doom that had been inflicted on no other human being, and by the results of which he had ceased to be human. Yet, withal, it seemed one of the most terrible consequences of that doom, that the victim no longer regarded it as a calamity, but had finally accepted it as the greatest good that could have befallen him."

It is this mark of favor that the Patient used to surround himself with faithful followers who found in him the sign of the prophet, the anointed one that spoke for the Almighty and guided them to their covenanted land historically preserved by the sacrificial blood of their ancestors shed in battles centuries ago, a manifest destiny that exonerated them from the laws of nature or society should the blood of innocents be shed to attain what had been granted to them by their God. He coddled this awareness by displaying religious fervor in wearing sacred emblems like the golden throat medallion stamped with the seal of Thorthana, the blue "R" sign of acceptance of the Almighty's ultimate power.

Now as the sun rises behind the black clouds on the seventh day of the sacred season and darkness covers the land, the Patient stirs to life in his own dark world oblivious to time itself since for him time no longer exists, only the endless absence of light and the intractable yet never ending memories that haunt his waking moments leaving him frustrated, humiliated and depressed. His mind navigates a circumscribed world that circles round and round continuously as though he's on an erratic merry go round grabbing futilely for the golden ring of meaning that time after time eludes his grasp.

Nothing in his experience mirrors now. Always his command brought results; always others did his bidding; always others fulfilled his desire; always his thinking went unquestioned. But now, now he lies motionless, un-acknowledged, a formless figure forgotten and abandoned, a meaningless mass of decaying flesh. His mind fights consciousness as the plague of memories infests his being, forcing him to contend with things already done, done years ago, forgotten long ago, resurrected now to torment him like blistering sores that itch, an unending agony no longer controlled by his calculating mind but subject to whim and unfathomable questioning.

He hears the door open quietly and listens as steps move toward his bed. He waits anxiously for the sound of Humilia's voice knowing it must be her since the entrance was made so softly. But she remains quiet as she approaches her Patient, carefully observing his frozen features and the immobile form. She checks the monitors before removing her coat and scarf, then hangs them in the nearby closet. She returns to his bedside, smoothes the sheet beneath his chin, and begins the ritual of bathing. As she moves about the room gathering the warm cloths from the heater and the fresh bedclothes, she hums one of her psalms. He responds spontaneously, emotionally as though she could hear him speaking to her.

Your gentle voice, my Angel, wakens this empty space as though the rising sun has broken over the hill ... light penetrating the darkest recesses of a cave. I live now to hear your sweet voice ... nothing else gives me hope in this hole that offers none ... just you, my unknown nurse, my Elusian nurse. Oh, my Angel, what irony is there, that you alone befriend the tormenter of your people. I would there were a time we might meet and I could tell you how much you mean to me in this life beyond death that I share with no one.

I think, when you are gone, that some monster greater than I designed this incredible torture that drowns me in my sins where I must muck around in a slough of my own creation ...and for some reason I cannot fathom, I must confront what I've done as though I'm facing my Divine who clasps the sacred book believing in it are the answers I'm forced to see. Yet my gut explodes at obeying what others teach and I reject what I'm forced to confront. What do you offer that makes me respond in kindness to one I should hate? I know only that you recognize I am, immobile yet breathing, dead to all yet alive to you. Talk to me, Humilia, talk to me.

As though in response to her Patient's agonizing plea, Humilia begins talking to the immobile form she now wheels into place beside the bathing sink.

"You know I just returned from Joyoa last night; I was gone all day. You may not have noticed. I'm sorry I had to leave. I don't like to have strangers attend you. They're always so rude. But I'll make up for it today. Carita will be here in a moment. We'll wash you in warm water with sweet smelling soap. You'll feel so much better. Oh, here's Carita now." Humilia's voice rose when she saw Carita who noticed that she was talking to the Patient.

"Are you talking to him again? If someone comes they'll think you are crazy." While Carita speaks in a joking way, her concern is not lost on Humilia.

"Do you know how sad it would be if he, all these months, could hear but could not tell us. Have you ever thought about that, about being alive yet buried in your own body. I can't deny that he might hear me, even need some human voice to give comfort or to make him feel he's not alone. Remember our psalm, 'Let us look upon each other as the source/of our salvation, for there is no other.' We're taught this, Carita, even if we must feel like fools before others. If he is as bad as they say, he needs our caring even more. I want so much for him to know I'm here, that he's not alone."

"Can you still say these things after being with your brother and father yesterday? I can't believe that they share your feelings. Both live the misery that this Patient inflicted on them and their friends. I want to hear what Ismaal said; he's in the midst of the worst of it. The news yesterday mentioned a family killed by a missile on the beach, the children, their mother and an uncle. They're investigating what happened, and all that means is that no one will be responsible. That's the way it is. We can't do anything about it, even the fanatics and those crazy with grief that kill themselves can't stop this slaughter. How can we battle tanks, planes, ships, bulldozers, missiles? It's like the rifle shot game at the side show only we're the targets, the sitting ducks. They even shoot at us when we throw stones." The acid in Carita's voice strains through her recital of the occupation revealing the depth of her anguish and resentment.

"Enough, Carita. I don't want to talk about these things right now. We have to bathe him. I promised him we'd be gentle. I have many things to tell you, but we must wait, please." Her words cloak the sadness that seeped through her desperate cry. Both girls feel the desperation that locks them inside the walls of the old city and, now, with Humilia's visit to Joyoa, the reverberation of that depression in the little hill town that used to be a refuge from the power of the occupying forces.

Carita's right, my Angel, she's right. I'm the treacherous one, the one you must fear. I learned early on not to love ... no one, not even God ... especially not God ... Self-love only. Love destroys power, robs the ruthless of his one ultimate weapon, indifference. I've denied love to all, family, neighbors, even Nefaria. That indifference is my shield; it needs only lies, deceit, and arrogance to keep it shining, beyond reproach. But you, Humilia, my caring Angel, know nothing of this, couldn't even contemplate it. Your innocence is in your simplicity. Your psalms promise what humans can never attain; they are the wishes the

powerful design to comfort the deprived.

Perhaps it is your innocence that makes me respond so deeply to you, perhaps it's because I know none will ever know what thoughts curse this living dead man compelling me to look into the eyes of indifference that mirrors the blackness of my soul. I do not know why you care for me, why you sing so sweetly to me, why you talk to me, why you show such kindness to the man who crippled your father.

Does your kindness grow in ignorance and innocence? Has no fear forced you to build walls of hate around your enemies? How different a world from mine where I live a prisoner in the jail I built. Now, when I should be dead, I lie in the blackness of thought that makes all else invisible and unreal; only my judgments acted upon and executed exist. There is no other reality now. No existence but unobstructed decisions already made, decisions that expelled hundreds of thousands from their homes, decisions that enabled heinous acts to advance my desires, decisions, decisions twisting in the wind and my eternal punishment, to weigh my identity as beast or saint. What retribution is this, to wallow in my barbaric past -- loveless, isolated, alienated from human kind – cursed to see through your eyes, the eyes of my victim! The ultimate incomprehensible irony of the fate I deny exists. To travel in the darkness of thought untouched by another destroys the only thing that gives meaning to my being, the idea of Nefaria that lived in me, lost now in the dark realms of silence where nothing grows, the palpable wasteland of human futility. I lived my life creating fear, blindly

assuming a right I would grant no person over me; now I exist in this surreal realm between life and death, the embodiment of fear. Such is the grave after life. Would you fear me, Humilia, if you knew who I am? ...

As the Patient suffers through his internal agony, the girls bathe him carefully, gently applying warm water, softly dabbing dry the wet skin, sprinkling fresh powder on his body, removing the soiled linens and replacing them with sweet smelling sheets. They then change his gown and tighten the outer cerecloth. Neither speaks. Humilia's cry stifled any talk about Joyoa.

****

But unbeknownst to Humilia and Carita the Patient falls into a deep sleep in the depths of which he finds himself surrounded by adulating crowds of Pilgrims standing on the steps of the capitol building, stretching as far as his eyes can see down Ypocrisis Street, all waving Nefarian flags, chanting the national anthem as bands play and balloons float above the masses into the deep blue sky of this glorious fall evening. He stands there beneath the cornice that displays in high relief images of the prophets turned in profile toward the center piece, the distinctive state seal of Nefaria, dressed in his general's white uniform garlanded with green and red sashes, epaulets and rows of colorful ribbons, a cluster of stars crowning the blue rim of his beaked hat as attendants flank him on either side each holding one of the banners symbolic of the seven days of the sacred season of forgiveness and retribution.

He thrusts his hands above his head pointing to the sky and smiles at the crowd, acknowledging their homage to him as the accepted leader of the Nefarian state.

As the music swells into a triumphant march on this seventh day of great victory, he descends the stairs to make his way out of the walls of the ancient city of Desperia and into the covenanted lands of Elusia, and the crowds part like waves providing him a colorful causeway down Ypocrisis Street. On either side, enormous images of him as a young soldier, as General, as a devout worshipper in the Assembly Hall, as a candidate for high office, as Defense Minister, as diplomat and, finally, as Prime Minister glow in the blue glass of the high rise buildings that line the street replacing the billboard images of beautiful girls, vacation homes by the sea, and beauty products usually displayed. The entire assembly moves in unison through the old city toward the eastern gate flowing like a river that ebbs and flows from side to side as the causeway continues to open in advance of the conquering general and his entourage. All bow humbly as he passes murmuring ancient prayers from the prophecies of Thorthana. He acknowledges their worshipful manner with a raised hand in benediction looking very much the regal Lord of the imperial state of Nefaria.

When he arrives at the eastern-most gate in the old walled city, the crowd slows respectfully to allow him to pass. The soldiers open the massive wooden planked gate that gapes beneath the parapets like a huge mouth; he passes through with the crowd following slowly, an elongated pulsing snake that slides past the open doors as he continues down the narrow alleys of Elusia, the same route that Humilia had taken when she went to Joyoa. His route now turns north running parallel to the new wall that he erected to enclose the Elusians. This gray monolith rises abruptly out of the alleyway, 25 feet high, blocking out everything to the west, including ancient sections of Elusia, now a part of Nefaria, buildings that had been home for Elusians for centuries lost forever to the encroaching Nefarians.

He turns toward the right going east up the steep hills crowded with dirty and decaying white blocked buildings stacked upon each other, housing for the thousands of Elusians jammed into this small patch of land. When he reaches the crest of the rise before it swings back toward the west, he turns to see the Pilgrims swarming through the streets, small black forms darting hither and thither, disappearing into side alleys and streets, flowing now up the hill through every crevice like vermin infesting an enormous refuse pile. He notices the black clouds forming in the west far over the city of Desperia and feels the cold wind lashing his face causing his eyes to water.

His triumphant parade through the streets turns menacingly into a funeral cortège where a slow mournful wail replaces the brilliant tone of the triumphant march, where deep purple and blue-black banners draping coffins pulled by mourners replace the bright white and blue flags and gold lined banners that billow in the morning breeze, and dark ominous clouds slink through the streets and alleyways both inside the old city and beyond its gates replacing the warm blue sky that glowed in the evening sun when he stood under the state seal on Ypocrisis Street.

Nothing prepared him for this horrific vision and

nothing he can do as he lies in his black tomb can stop its ineluctable sway over his dreaming mind. Fear envelopes him, a fear far worse than the adrenalin rush of battle, fear that sears the soul with the indelible mark of the traitor, known now in his heart as the reality of his life, never to be forgotten, never to be forgiven, ever to be the icon of betrayal, treachery, and ridicule.

But the nightmare continues. As he climbs the hills of east Elusia, skeletons waving the green banner of the Elusian people stream out of the houses that line the streets; they join the cortege that pulls the coffins, a train of coffins that moves up the hill from the gate below each carried by cowled figures, three to a side, all chanting a sorrowful dirge that hovers as threateningly above the scene as the black clouds that now envelop Desperia. A black pall descends over all the land from the walls of the old city and over every hill and valley in Elusia. His dream becomes the reality of his existence; in his comatose body, he's become the image of Elusia, the barren, impotent, discarded land that he has turned into a wasteland teeming with hordes of humans who seek solace, comfort, joy, and hope, but live in suffering, imprisonment, injustice and helplessness, a people lost on the world's stage, victims of indifference, malice, racism and fear.

But as he crests the top of the hill that looks north toward Joyoa, he turns once again to observe the strange scene spread out below him, a dark loathsome scene where Pilgrims swarm like maggots, crawling over the skeletons, the emptied houses and streets and byways that stagger up the hill toward the Patient; the banners of the sacred days they hold aloft, ripped now by the blistering wind, snap in the cold air oblivious to their sacred significance.

He sees through the heavy fog that envelopes the hills, he hears the weeping and wailing of the cowled figures who bare the coffins of the Elusian dead, he stares in disbelief as the entombment wall he's erected looms over him as though it had wrenched loose from its foundations and marches forward, coming closer as the moments pass. He turns in fright from this funereal scene and looks to Joyoa. There in the distance to the east, the sun glints through the black sky, a sliver at first, but it grows as he watches the landscape slowly come into view. To the right and to the left the enormous gray wall stretches as far as he can see converging in the sun's glare on the horizon. Then, suddenly, it too appears to move as he stands transfixed on this crest from which he can see the ancient city of Desperia and the barren wastes of Elusia. But as the wall moves towards him, it blocks out the sun throwing shadows over all the land, casting a dark shroud over his mind as though it had no light to illuminate his world, destroying forever his dreams of a resurrected Nefaria and his aspirations to eternal glory as Emperor.

The horror of the scene surrounds him now on every side; the walls move like sidewinders closing in on him, growing in size as they sweep over distant hills and down into the valleys pushing trees, houses, bushes, stones and sand before their massive bulk, ever closer, ever larger, high menacing, cement monstrosities that turn day into night, burying alive all inside. And he stands frozen before this implacable force fearing his ultimate end; helpless, he glances back at Desperia just as it sinks beneath the sand in a thunderous roar of lashing wind and hail. He stares in disbelief as he watches the Pilgrims slide backward, down the streets and alleys, arms flailing, legs slipping beneath them as they see the gaping cavity created by the sink hole that forms under the weight of the wall and into which Desperia slips where billowing clouds of dust belch forth from below, and he hears the wailing cries of all the faithful as they hurtle toward the abyss that beckons the legions of Pilgrims to their everlasting doom.

Now in absolute terror, he turns suddenly to the east only to confront the wall as it encircles him, its gray mass towering above him as he searches for the light in the evening sky. But all has turned to darkness as he lowers his eyes to confront his own visage in the mirrored wall in front of him, a mirror that reflects the horrid scene behind him and the heinous face that stares back at him, for there in that massive mirror he sees the crown of Nefaria on top of his gray hair that sticks out over his ears, the crown of ancient wisdom worn these many centuries by all the kings and prophets of past civilizations, ensconced on his skull, his eye sockets sunk deep into the bone, black, ominous, blind to the reality they allegedly observe, and, most horrendous of all, his mouth, swarming with maggots, a gaping hole laid back in a terrible sneer as though he laughs at himself, nay, mocks himself - the icon of clownish diversion, the butt of ridicule and savage sterility. In that moment he realizes he is witness within his own grave of his corrupted self, the ultimate end of all his acts, the final quintessential glory of his horrifying journey through life, when suddenly the mirrored wall towering over him cracks in a thousand places piercing the ever tightening walls of his tomb as the shovel's dirt cascades onto his coffin and all goes silent.

His mind erupts in horrifying terror, the vision imprinted indelibly on his consciousness. Time may not exist in his frozen isolation, but for the first time he feels a future, undefined perhaps, yet marked with the existential threat of Thorthana's prophecy of ultimate retribution.

Humilia! My Angel, where are you? I've suffered such a dream, a hellish vision seared into my soul so deeply ... my life now, reduced to unending reflection, transforms me into an image of human depravity, decades of days devoted to destruction, desolation and death, the sum purpose of my being ... I cannot recall a day when I did not cause the death or torture or demolition of an Elusian life. I travel now in this hellish pit through fields of Elusian dead, their bodies form moguls on which I walk, their eyes staring up at me in disbelief and, yet, with sorrow for me. I move through fields of loss where the air stirs, surrounding me like the gentle pulse of a person's breath, the breath of life never lived. Nightmarish visions of countless days of thinking without interruption ... mutilated faces stare at me, children, children as far as I can see shrouded in the shadows of the massive gray wall, never to see the sun, or know the thrill of running through the hills of Elusia ... to have to live in this rumination of my atrocities hour upon hour, to face the punishment of the Almighty, to see and feel the pain and suffering I have inflicted on others ... that is a hell beyond comprehension ... to live to remember and never die, to relive the insidious toxic beliefs I've infested our children with that will be their inheritance forever, a mental and emotional tomb in which they live every day of their life. And, God forbid, to never speak to another, to confess to those deceived and destroyed, to bear witness to this understanding in the awful silence of this vault where I

lie alone, the sole arbiter of my acts - without comfort, without compassion, without forgiveness, without end. Oh, God, Humilia, what have I done?

Even as her Patient laments the agony of his abandonment, his awful, never ending torment, the ever recurring images of his brutality toward the Elusians flows forth from some unexplainable depth within, where despair and hopelessness reside, and he cries out to Humilia to talk to him, to sing to him, to touch him, to forgive him that he may rest, relieved of the horrific retribution thrust upon him.

But while Humilia cannot see his torment, she feels the anguishing cry that tears at his mind unable to erupt from his throat, the ancient wail of all who suffer beyond the ears of their sisters and brothers, lost, forgotten, the dying detritus of human waste, known to none, abandoned and forlorn in the shifting sand where even the wind whines like a banshee's cry drowning the lone lament of the suffering Patient in the abyss into which Nefaria sinks to become only the last of all the glorious empires that live and die in these middle kingdoms where human desire and greed meet their ineluctable end.

The end

Postscript

On March 4th, 2007, I published an article in *MWC News* out of Canada titled "Buried Alive: Life Inside the Entombment Wall," a polemic on the plight of the Palestinian people living in occupied territory. The article decried the absence of conscience that has attended the 60 years of oppression inflicted on the Palestinians by the Israelis, an absence of human concern, not only by the Israelis, but by the entire developed world including most importantly the United States. *MWC News* puts the conscience back in the news.

The remaining portion of this "Postscript" revisits that article because it was the inspiration for this book, *The Chronicles of Nefaria: a Morality Tale.* The closing paragraph notes the irony of Prime Minister Ariel Sharon, as he slipped into a coma, (a condition he is still in as this book is written), and the condition he imposed on the Palestinian people by entombing them inside his Wall, the cement encasement in which the coffin is placed.

Sharon's comatose state, essentially dead to the world, mirrors the condition he inflicted on the Palestinians. He became for me a metaphor of all those who seek power to inflict their will on the innocent, to impose their idea on the frightened masses, and in the process acquire great wealth, prestige, and historical presence as they write the books that extol their own virtues, and all the while, as the days and years pass it is the innocent who lie in their graves forgotten.

This work is allegorical, intentionally so, as it records the actions of a man, of necessity fictionalized, to represent all, who in my lifetime, imaged the most reprehensible characteristics of human kind, embodied in this gallery of monsters: Hitler, Franco, Mussolini, Stalin, Chiang Kai Chek, Pol Pot, the Shah, Pinochet, Milosevic, Kim Jung Il, Hussein, and George W. Bush. I see in Israel under Ariel Sharon a nation driven by deceit, a veritable General Demas, who leads a wicked nation, Nefaria, to enslave and ethnically cleanse the people of another state, turned under his regime into a barren wasteland, Elusia, the visible image of Palestine. Unfortunately in this fictionalized world, Ariel must confront the actions he has performed in life simply because he has been left immobile yet able to think, forced to relive his life in the presence of goodness, a kind and sweet girl, a victim of his brutality, Humilia, from Joyoa, a small town in the occupied territories. .

As he lies helpless in his thoughts, the Nefarian people (Israelis, Christian Zionists, etc.) live on oblivious to his agony, enveloped in their beliefs imaged in the Sacred Season of Forgiveness and Retribution. For seven days we listen to his memory and his mind confront his day to day actions and we witness a man of power tackle his life in reflection, an atypical behavior for one in his position. Indeed, that is his suffering, his eternal hell.

Post-Modernism recognizes the instability of words, the indefiniteness of identity, the illusions that we construct to give us significance. Who is to say who Sharon is and what he might have been? Where is Nefaria or Elusia? In what chapter of history do we not run across them? Why is it we know how life should be, what is good and what is bad, yet turn these words inside out, and rarely witness humans acting morally? Perhaps that is the purpose of stories, to wile away the time lest we are forced to live the reality.

****

Life Inside the Entombment Wall

"The worst sin towards our fellow creatures is not to hate them, but to be indifferent to them; that's the essence of inhumanity." **(George Bernard Shaw, *The Devil's Disciple*, ACT II)**

Terrorists struck once again in Jenin this past week killing four, wounding twenty-eight civilians, including two journalists and four children and women. Fifty five civilians were kid napped including six children. Three buildings used for agriculture were destroyed and 199 donums of agricultural land confiscated. Other attacks occurred in Far'oun village where six homes were demolished that stood too close to the Wall. Terrorists beat civilians in Bal'ein village, west of Ramallah who were protesting the demolitions and the extension of the Wall. The attacks continue, unreported in the United States since they are carried out by our allies, the Israeli Defense Forces.

Despite the deafening silence that accompanies the on-going construction of the illegal Wall, declared such by the

International Court of Justice, despite staged non violent demonstrations in Bal'ein, Jayous, Bethlehem, Ramallah's Bil'in village and elsewhere through out the West Bank, despite the outcry this week raised by Sinn Fein's International Affairs spokesperson, Aengus O Snodeigh against the mounting atrocities committed by the Jews on the Palestinians, those who have a conscience, both international and Israeli, stand in the streets chanting and singing that the wall will fall and freedom will come to the Palestinian people. But no one listens. Instead, "a large contingent of Israeli forces, including soldiers, police and border guards, began assaulting the nonviolent demonstrators with rifle butts and truncheons." (Palestinian Center for Human Rights, 22-24 February, 2007).

Indifference, Shaw tells us, is the essence of inhumanity; it is worse than hatred precisely because it does not recognize the living, breathing brother and sister who suffer the agony inflicted on them by a people who proclaim to be civilized even as they inflict bestial and barbaric acts on the helpless. That makes the citizens of the world worse sinners than the IDF and the Jews in Israel who tolerate the racist hatred that drives their government. Indifference costs nothing, requires no judgment, raises no principles, imposes no action, causes no discomfort; it is the void that rests in a soul that cares only for self and nothing for its fellow man. It is the beast that John describes in *The Secret Book* (11:4-5): "The rulers brought Adam into the shadow of death so that they might produce a figure again, but now from earth, water, fire, and the spirit that comes from matter, that is, from the ignorance of darkness, and desire, and their own contrary spirit. This figure is the tomb, the newly created body that these criminals put on the human as a fetter of forgetfulness." The indifferent finds recourse in all that satisfies self, all that pleases the body – drink, food, pandering – and all that pleases the desires – gold, silver, presents – and so isolates self from the world that might disturb that absorption lost in forgetfulness. Should that isolated world be threatened, the fear aroused against such a person – terror, servility, anguish and shame – locks them in even more.

That fear can be triggered by those in power. It is a tool used to control the conscience of a people. Arthur Miller wrote about it in *The Crucible*, a play about the Salem witch trials of 1692. Citizens threatened by fear for self, even in the form of invisible forces determined to exist by their ministers, blindly accept what they cannot know and become accomplices to the criminal acts of their leaders. They have literally turned their individual consciences over to their government. That is the case in Israel. The Wall is the visible icon of an invisible threat created by Sharon's administration to accomplish a political end, the confiscation of Palestinian land and the psychological death of the Palestinian people. The Wall is built of fear in order to engender fear in both the Israelis who see themselves as victims once more, and in the Palestinians who see themselves entombed, without hope, without compassion, without justice. Indeed, the Wall rises in all its grotesque grayness like the cement box into which a coffin is placed, and in its image casts a pall over the people of Palestine that suffocates their spirit even as it separates brothers from sisters, children from parents, friends from families, making impossible a normal life. How can one people inflict such heinous conditions on another? How can the people of America sit idly by while their representatives cow-tow to the dictates of AIPAC and the world looks on in disbelief. What has become of the America that cares for the tired and the poor?

Consider what Sharon and now Olmert have constructed. The Wall rests entirely within Palestine while it snakes over hills and valleys, down the middle of streets, carves towns and villages into parts separating people who have lived together for decades, centuries even, confiscates to the Israeli side the aquifers and wells belonging to the people of Palestine, as well as the olive groves and crops belonging to the people, and the arable land that will become the settlers fields and additional settlements for those who never lived a day in Palestine and have no history here, no memories, no culture that is indigenous if two thousand years is considered a measure. Completely surrounded, without access to their fields or mosques or friends or hospitals or employment, they have but two choices, leave or die. They are indeed buried alive by the Jews, a fate less absolute than the gas chamber since they can choose to leave, and leave behind two thousand years of history and land that has given life to generations of family embodied in 1000 year old olive trees summarily ripped from the ground by Israeli bulldozers, leave mosques in which they have worshiped decade upon decade, and leave their memories as those driven from their homes in 1947 lost theirs when their towns were razed and all that had been was no more.

Or they die; a living death that drags on day after day in poverty and need, dependent on those not indifferent to their plight: Israelis that have not capitulated to the wanton waste of human life because they know what victim hood is and recognize it; friends from all countries of the world who care enough to come as witnesses to the humiliation, the degradation, the racism that permeates the settlers and is embodied in the Israeli government; Jews from around the world who decry the inhumanity inflicted by their own on another; and Americans who care because they have faced the same threatened fear that enabled a corrupt and amoral administration to invade and occupy countries against international law. That is their fate.

Ironically, the conditions imposed on the Palestinians in their tomb, the benumbed state of their being, the years upon years of isolation and alienation, the loss of sensitivity to the rising and setting of the sun, the loss of friends and family, the loss of consciousness to all that surrounds them since it has been turned to ashes and waste, the loss of memory that gave identity to their being since none know now that they even exist behind the Wall, the loss of their very purpose to live, the loss of hope that has been entombed with them, their dependency on strangers to sustain what life breathes in their lungs is mirrored in the metaphor of Sharon lying in his sheeted shroud as day crowds on day, unable to respond to anyone or anything, entombed in his own flesh, unconscious, as the indifferent are unconscious, to his own plight or that of those he has buried alive.

****

Critics will quibble with the unnecessary intrusion of allegory when the narrative clearly focuses on a living man and his years as Prime Minister of Israel. But in our Post-Modern world there is clearly no distinction between fictional devices and reality. We've put the illusion aside if only to show that the more gripping reality portrayed heretofore in fiction is only made possible by the tricks of the trade. Here we include them to blunt the feelings of the overly sensitive; let them choose to hide in fiction lest the evil of our world propel them into the slough of despond.

Other writers in other times drew inspiration from ancient kings and emperors; indeed, Shakespeare created his greatest masterpieces by bringing the dead back to life, Caesar, Cleopatra, Henry, Richard. Yet his purpose was to reflect on these images as they mirrored the reality in his own day. Why, I would ask, not use what is at hand, if in the mirror, they reflect a finer image of human degradation than the emperors of old? I look at our world, the last sixty years of the 20th century, the years of my life, and I realize the barbarity inflicted by our leaders surpassed that of all prior centuries. I had dreams that this new century would usher in a time of peace and understanding, yet we live now, even in this first decade, only a continuation of the past and a prophecy of unending war waged by those in the west who claim to represent the advanced civilizations on the planet. Why resurrect images from the past? Have we not the very essence of allegorical evil resident in the Prime Minister of Nefaria and the Emperor of the United Corporate States? Let their respective shadows fall over the wastelands they have created in their arrogance that we may learn and dream once again.